THE BRIDES
WORE SPURS

BARRY BONNER

authorHOUSE®

AuthorHouse™ LLC
1663 Liberty Drive
Bloomington, IN 47403
www.authorhouse.com
Phone: 1-800-839-8640

Published by AuthorHouse 06/28/2014

ISBN: 978-1-4969-2048-5 (sc)
ISBN: 978-1-4969-2049-2 (e)

Also by Barry Bonner

MURDEROUS HUMOR

SAVAGE MEN, SAVAGE EARTH

BLACK DIAMONDS

PARADE OF FOOLS

Available through AuthorHouse
or your local bookstore.

This one's for
MIKE & LORRIE

CHAPTER ONE

The West of the 1880s was "cattle heaven" and cowboys "angels on horseback"—sort of. There were millions of acres of lush grasslands from Texas to Missouri; Nebraska to North Dakota; Arizona to Montana; Colorado to Wyoming. And in the middle of Wyoming set the McKenna ranch; huge and prosperous—thousands of acres—half owned outright, and half leased; a home to 5,000 cattle and hundreds of horses. Two thousand beef steers had been shipped to the Kansas City stockyards in the recent fall roundup. The steers had been fat and sassy and the price for beef had been fat and sassy as well.

The three McKenna brothers—Eden, Boone, and Mason—were more than satisfied, but that was soon to change. Once the fall roundup was done and the hectic, sweaty work ended, the brothers soon had a lot of spare time on their hands—quiet time. All but two of the fourteen regular cowhands had been paid off and let go until spring. Chunk Bascom and Billy Birdsong remained to help out when needed, living ten miles from the ranch at the old line shack, keeping an eye on the cattle and horses that grazed freely over the rolling waves of buffalo grass.

The brothers were batching it at the large main house when a laziness began to creep in like a thin fog off the silent prairie. It hadn't been too long since their Pa had died, then Ma followed shortly after; some said of a broken heart. But Ma would have told you it was from overwork, and glad to be done with it. There was the constant cooking, cleaning and scrubbing of the main house, bunkhouse; the laundry chores, sewing for all the ranch hands, then extra hours thrown in for doctoring the sick, or the unfortunate who got crippled up by a mean cow or vicious bronc. It had all become a stone anchor around her neck. No, Ma's heart didn't have nothing to do with it; she simply got wore down to a stub. So they put her to bed with a pick and shovel, and lots and lots of prairie flowers.

The brothers soon came to realize that it was one thing to be out cowboying, drinking in town, and the occasional barroom brawl; but it was about as much fun as a funeral when the household chores reared up in their faces like a snorting outlaw stallion.

Things in the main house went from bad to more than worse. Dust and dirt began to accumulate at a noticeable rate. Things didn't get put away very good; it was easier to just let it lie were it fell. Dishes, pots, and pans, knives, forks, and spoons didn't get washed as good as Ma used to do it. And somehow dirty clothes piled up in scattered mounds like a prairie dog town. But the worst of it was the cooking. The brothers had agreed to take turns to relieve the hatred they had towards the job. However, the situation around the cook stove deteriorated rapidly. It was like they had a contest going to see who could come up with the worst grub. Sometimes it tasted as if it hadn't been prepared by human hands.

Eden, Boone, and Mason began kicking themselves for letting Sorehead Jones, the chuck wagon cook go. True he was married to the bottle, and when he was stewed to the gills it was easier talking Chinese to a pack mule until sorehead got sober. There was also the money issue. Sorehead pulled down sixty dollars a month as hash slinger, while the regular hands drew thirty a month, and the brothers, always with an eye for improving their finances, thought Sorehead's pay would fit better in their pocket than his. They told themselves it was like finding money in the street. Now, however, they would have paid sixty a week for the same irritating, tobacco spitting demon they had been glad to be rid of. He didn't smell too good neither.

Though the brothers were determined to persevere in their predicament, things went downhill faster than a wagonload of cannonballs. No matter if they fried, baked, boil, stewed, chopped, mashed it, singed it or burned it, the grub was hard to choke down even with a couple swallows of coffee—thick as tar and tasting like it.

Then one evening, just before supper time, the brothers sat in gloomy silence in front of the large fireplace in the parlor, staring dismally into the leaping flames, their stomachs growling.

Eden, the oldest brother, gave a soft sigh as the glow of the fire played on the strong chiseled features of his face darkened by the sun and weather. His curly black hair shined and his eyes were bold looking. He was the ramrod of the outfit and his tall muscular frame had a self-assured, confident aura about it. Here was a man unafraid of tackling anything—almost.

"Whose turn to cook?" asked Eden.

Boone and Mason gave him a quick glance and stared into the fire.

Boone shook his head and said, almost to himself, "Just ain't got the stomach for it."

He was the second oldest, and just as handsome as Eden and Mason; slimmer, but equally hard muscled, and could ride anything he cinched his saddle to. For all his ruggedness has was a man who was respectful to others, and there was a gentle confidence to his voice. He had piercing eyes set in a smooth tanned face that most of the time had a crooked, devilish smile on it, but not right now.

"Well, I ain't got the stomach for it neither," said Mason.

He was the youngest, and took after Boone in looks and long, lean body. His broad smile and burning brown eyes always made the young girls turn their heads for a second look; as did his black wild-looking hair. His temper was short when it came to men, but mild and meek when it came to the pretty ladies.

"We can't sit here and starve," said Eden in a gruff tone.

"It'd be easier than eatin' that grub you fixed this mornin'," replied Boone.

Eden started to say something, thought better of it, and chalked up Boone's grumpiness to the torment of hunger pains.

"Should have never let Sorehead go," mumbled Mason.

"I wish you'd quit saying that," said Eden.

"Mason's right," said Boone. "I'd give the saddle off my horse to have him here, right now."

"I'll throw in mine, too," added Mason. "Them steaks you cooked last night are still churning in my belly."

"If you can burn anything better, go out and fire up the stove," replied Boone, insulted.

"I apologize, Boone," said Mason, softly. "I shouldn't have said that. I should have said, them steaks was tougher than a saddle blanket."

Boone turned his head quickly, eyebrows raised, but voice low. "You better hobble your lips, cowboy."

"That's enough," said Eden. "We can't sit here all night degradin' each other."

Eden walked to the fireplace, leaned his hands against the mantle and began to think. Boone and Mason watched.

"What's on your mind?" Boone asked.

"No way around it," replied Eden, "got to find us a cook, no matter what the cost."

"Money be damned," said Boone, loudly.

"When do we start?" asked Mason, eager as Boone.

"First thing in the mornin'," replied Eden. "We cinch up and head for town, and pray we can come up with somebody."

"If not," said Boone, "at least we can get something decent to eat."

CHAPTER TWO

The sun was just a faint glow on the horizon when the brothers entered the main corral and roped their best traveling horse—barrel-chested, long-legged, and could run like a scared deer. The boys weren't about to waste time getting to where they wanted to go. It was forty miles to town, and they were anticipating a mouth-watering breakfast, and an easy search for a cook—come hell or high water.

They were about to step up into the saddle when they heard dogs barking. A man's voice mingled faintly among the yipping cries. The brothers climbed onto the corral rails and squinted into the pale gray dawn and were able to make out a black mound of something coming in their direction.

It wasn't long before a large wagon, pulled by two odd-looking, short-legged mules, became distinct. Squirming around in the rear of the wagon were ten dogs of all sizes, shapes and colors. Seated on the wide wagon seat was a tall stick of a man. His matted gray hair hung down past his shoulders. His matching long beard hung clear to his waist, and looked as if he'd been using it as a napkin. Dark, greasy buckskins clung to him like they were wet with water. And the fringe on the sleeves and pants were long and tattered, as were the soft moccasin boots tied to his stick legs. For a hat—that wasn't really a hat—was a square piece of wolf hide held in place by a long leather thong, tied under his chin. A short piece of wolf's tail hung to one side.

Eden, Boone, and Mason gazed in wonder as they sat atop the corral watching this strange apparition move towards them. With uninhibited gusto, the man was singing a song, and the words didn't make any sense whatsoever; which was fine, as the baying, howling canine choir drowned out any semblance of meaning—if there was any.

The wagon came to a stop beside the brothers, and the two sad looking mules heaved a sigh of relief and bowed their heads. The man in buckskin ended his nonsense song with a flourish of his long, thin hand, and the dogs fell silent. The brothers sat grinning, as did the man in buckskin.

"A happy day to you, gentlemen," said the man. "Dog Kelly's the name. Buffalo's my game."

5

"Don't see much buffalo around this territory anymore," said Mason.

"And it breaks my heart," replied Kelly. "As well as my purse."

"But you can still sing some, sounds like," said Boone.

"I'm happy as a mouse in a wheel of cheese, cowboy."

"Well, step on down and rest yourself," said Eden, smiling.

"That include the boys?"

"Boys?" said Eden.

Kelly motioned to the dogs.

"And the boys, too," said Eden.

Kelly leaped from the wagon, and the ten dogs weren't far behind. They surrounded him and eyed his every move.

"There's feed in the barn for your mules," began Eden, "and feed in the main house for yourself."

"My boys have to eat too, you know."

"Help your self," replied Eden.

"You won't join us?" said Kelly, disappointed.

"Headed for town," answered Boone.

"But I wouldn't feel right, me and my boys eatin' your grub without repaying you."

"Don't worry about it," said Mason, as he and his brothers climbed down from the corral.

"But I insist on fixing you a meal fit for a king," said Kelly.

The brothers stared at him then glanced at each other. Eden took a step forward eyeing Kelly carefully.

"You cook good, do you?" said Eden, cautiously.

"I can cook anything with meat on it, and it'll melt in your mouth, sir."

The brothers turned to one another, smiling like Cheshire cats. The words, "Ask and ye shall receive," passed silently between them.

The first few days went as smooth as silk, then a disappointing sourness set in. It wasn't that Dog Kelly had lied about his cooking, it was—well, he never changed clothes; never took them off; and he never bathed, stating it was not the right time. Summer was best. But summer was a long way off. He did all his cooking and other chores with his wide cartridge belt strapped around his skinny waist, and a long-bladed hunting knife tucked in on one side and a heavy old revolver tucked in on the other. His boys never left his side, and when he rolled up in his buffalo robe at night—in the middle of the kitchen floor, the boys formed a tight, furry circle around him. Kelly would hum a soothing lullaby until all were asleep, including himself. That's when strange sounds erupted. First, there was Kelly, mouth wide open, gargling and choking as if about to give up the ghost. Then the boys put up a chorus of low growling, sighing, sneezing and hammering of hind legs against the floor as the battle of fleas and ticks ensured. The kitchen windows rattled slightly in their worn pine frames.

Soon Kelly was lagging behind in the housekeeping and laundry. And despite his bragging how he was a whiz with needle and thread, he never seemed to get any of the brothers clothes mended, or for that matter the soles of his own moccasin boots which were coming apart at the seams.

It didn't take his boys long to makes themselves to home—acting like they'd been born and raised there. You couldn't find a place were there wasn't a dog stretched out on his side, belly, or back.

Eden, Boone, and Mason bit their lip and remained silent, but sullen, not wanting to offend the cook. There was an old saying among cowboys: "Only a fool argues with a skunk, a pack mule, or the cook." But that philosophy was wearing thin.

At breakfast, one morning, Kelly accidentally dropped a chunk of raw bacon on the floor and the fight was on. One of the boys grabbed it and took off like a streak of proverbial lightning, determined to keep the morsel for himself. The rest of the pack had opposing ideas and went after him, yelping like starving coyotes. Since there was a nipping frost that early in the morning none of the ranch house doors were open, so the steeple chase was held indoors. The boys were leaping and lunging over chairs, benches, and tables. A wild dash went in one room and out the other. Kelly had tears in his eyes from laughing at all the fun. And he encouraged his savage brood no end; howling long and hard like he was a blood relative.

Eden, Boone, and Mason sat at the long kitchen table forcing themselves not to look, and stuffing in the big breakfast Kelly had fixed—it was too good to stop and take time to beat or shoot any of the boys. But when the stampede of snapping, furry fiends took a short cut along the length of the kitchen table top, scattering plates, cups and eating utensils, the brothers did some snarling of their own.

Eden sprang to his feet, spurs ringing as he began cussing and yelling while the boys made another wild tour of the entire house. In the meantime, Boone flung open the kitchen door, hollering and motioning for the dogs to get the hell out. Mason began throwing whatever plates and cups he could lay hands on, but they ricocheted harmlessly off wet noses and bushy tails, and hackled backs.

Kelly was still enjoying the show when the dog with the bacon saw the open door and made his escape. The rest of the pack stayed with him, piling through the doorway in snarling hot pursuit.

With the baying of the hounds fading in the distance, Eden, Boone, and Mason gazed slowly around them. The huge kitchen looked as if a barrel of gunpowder had exploded. After surveying the destruction, the brothers turned to each other knowing exactly what had to be done. The three moved slowly towards Kelly, their spurs making a slow, ominous ring with each step. Kelly, still having a fine time, stood in the doorway, smiling and encouraging the boys as they raced in a dusty circle around the big bunkhouse.

"Looks like it's time to be movin' on," said Eden, fighting to control his temper.

"Yeah," said Kelly, still grinning at the boys. "They sure can move all right."

The brothers looked at each other.

"Dog, I'm talkin' about you," said Eden forcefully. "Time to cinch up and ride on."

"And quick," added Boone.

Kelly roared with laughter as the boys streaked past in the direction of the barn. "Look at 'em go," he said proudly.

"It's like talkin' to a corpse," said Mason.

"Got cotton for brains, all right," said Boone.

"So do we for hirin' him," added Eden. "Your ears workin', Dog?"

Kelly whirled around to face them, eyes large and wild. The brothers took a step back not knowing if he was going to grab his knife or revolver or both.

"Hear that?" said Kelly in a whisper.

"Yeah, we hear them damn dogs," replied Eden.

"No," said Kelly. "The rumblin'. I hear the good sound, the good rumblin'."

Kelly turned and walked outside, listening, his wild eyes scanning the endless, windy prairie.

"We better get out guns," said Boone, softly.

Eden held up a hand, stopping him, and walked towards Kelly. Boone and Mason followed, but not too close.

Kelly began laughing and dancing a little jig. "They're comin'. I knew they would. They're back."

"What the hell you talkin' about?" asked Eden.

The buffalo. Listen to 'em. Thunderin' through the deep grass, makin' that beautiful music like they always do."

"I don't hear nothin'." said Mason.

Kelly leaped into the air and ran for the barn, then stopped and turned. "I almost forgot," he yelled. "I quit!"

"Thank God," said the brothers.

It wasn't long before Kelly and the boys were whooping it up as his old worn out wagon, and scruffy mules, were racing away from the ranch; the mules braying as loud as Dog Kelly.

"Even his mules are loony," said Mason, still watching the frantic departure.

Eden and Boone, however, were staring into the kitchen.

"Looks like Custer's last stand," said Boone. "I'll get a shovel."

"Hold on," ordered Eden. "I ain't never had a horse throw me to the ground, and I ain't lettin' this do it either."

"What'll we do, burn the kitchen?" asked Boone.

"Mason," said Eden, "get our gunbelts, hats and coats, while me and Boone saddle the horses."

"Where we goin'?" asked Mason.

"To town. We're goin' to get us that cook if we have to kidnap one."

CHAPTER THREE

From a distance the town of Sweet Grass was a long dark gash in the middle of the treeless prairie. It was thriving handsomely due to the huge ranches and the cowboys who worked them. The Union Pacific Railroad was only one hundred miles away and was planning on building a spur road right to the center of Sweet Grass. New homes and stores were being built almost every week now. There was even a new three story hotel, and two sprawling boarding houses, and two churches—populated sparsely on Sundays. A litter of twenty saloons stood open day and night, seven days a week; some had dance halls, some extra large gambling dens, because in the fall and winter a lot of the cowboys moved to town. After wearing themselves out in roundups and cattle drives, the money bulging their pockets disappeared like handfuls of flour in a windstorm. There were lots of women to help them spend it—all shapes, sizes and colors, and of all occupations from A to Z.

But Eden and his brothers were only interested, right now, in the letters C—cook, and D—drink. Dismounting in front of the Prancing Rooster saloon, they tied their horses to the hitching rail, and glanced around at the noise and activity of the lively community that never seemed to sleep. It was a drastic change from the lonesome ranch they had left hours before; where the sound of the wind through the waving grass was a constant companion.

Mark it up to fate or rotten luck, the brothers had only taken three steps towards the saloon when Bronco Charlie seemed to drop out of the sky at their feet. Actually, he had been tossed out through the saloon doors and rolled down the steps. His shirt and pants were thread bare, his sheepskin coat had holes in the elbows, and his hat looked as if a herd of steers had stampeded across it and back again. Little tuffs of white hair showed just above his ears. Distinctive bowed legs proved he had done more riding then walking, and when he did walk he was a little stooped over from being piled on the ground once too often by a vicious bronc. That's why his thin lips were always pressed together in a perpetual grimace. He had been pretty well battered over the length of his lifetime, and had the scars and broken bones to prove it, along with a wrinkled, puffy face, big flat nose and bent ears. He was a cocky little stump made of thick arms and thick legs of a born bronc rider—who had seen far better days.

As Bronco struggled to his feet, Eden and Boone helped him and began dusting him off. Bronco smiled in thanks—he had just enough teeth left to chew a little beef and beans, and gnaw a soft biscuit now and then, but he was more attracted to liquids.

"You okay, cowboy?" Eden asked.

"Much obliged, fellas," replied Bronco. "Must have tripped comin' out the door?"

"Sure looked like it," said Boone.

"Ain't you Bronco Charlie?" said Mason, staring hard.

Bronco straightened noticeably. "And proud of it, son. I used to be the…" He squinted back at Mason, then Boone, then Eden. His face and eyes lit up bright and shiny. "You're the McKenna boys," he said loudly.

"It's sure been a while," said Eden as he and the others began shaking hands with Bronco.

"I remember you breakin' horses for Pa," said Boone.

"You boys was just little lumps when I did that," replied Bronco.

"Pa always said you was the best," said Mason.

"Your Pa was a smart man. Sorry to hear of his passin'. Say let's have a drink for old times sake."

"You sure that's a good idea?" said Eden.

"Huh?" said Bronco, puzzled.

"You look pretty well oiled now," said Boone.

"I do?" said Bronco, surprised.

"I remember you stayin' all winter with us one time," said Mason. "Ma was ailin', and you did all the cookin'."

"That's right I did. But that don't make me no less of a cowboy. I remember down in the Missouri Breaks country, I…"

"Hang on a minute," interrupted Boone. "I just had an idea."

Boone motioned for Eden and Mason to follow him, and walked off a few yards.

"What's up?" whispered Mason.

"Let's hire him," said Boone.

"For what?" asked Eden.

"Cookin'," replied Boone.

"Did you take a good look at him?" said Mason.

11

"That don't mean nothin'," said Boone. "He's just a cowboy down on his luck. Could be us standin' there someday."

"Well, he was pretty good at slingin' hash that winter," said Mason, glancing at Bronco.

"What do you think?" Boone asked Eden.

Eden threw a glance at Bronco slouched against the hitching rail. "I don't know," he said apprehensively. "That was a long time ago."

"So what?" said Boone. "Besides we can't turn our backs on one of Pa's old waddies."

"I side with Boone," said Mason.

The three looked at Bronco as he now reclined against the steps to the saloon, scratching his rear end as hard as he could.

"Have to give him a bath and some clean clothes," said Eden, still not convinced he should do it.

"Bet he'd work cheap, too," said Mason.

"Couldn't be any worse than Dog Kelly," said Boone.

"God forbid," said Eden.

Bronco stood up and smiled as Eden and his brother came towards him. "So what's cookin', boys?"

"You are," replied Eden.

"Huh?"

As Bronco listened to Eden's job offer, he scratched his head, chest, and every other place he could reach. The position of chief cook and bottle washer sounded like a lot of work, and none of it from the back of a horse. He hesitated until he realized his prospects for the future were slim to non-existent. His face flashed into an almost toothless grin as he made up his mind.

"Deal. Let's drink on it."

By the time Bronco had finished celebrating his good luck he had spent half of his thirty dollars wages Eden had advanced him. He was then escorted to his horse, tied into the saddle, and was led away to his new vocation.

CHAPTER FOUR

The next day, after a long, hot bath and his old clothes burned, Bronco proved himself to still be an A-1 hash slinger. Eden had set aside his apprehensions, and the brothers ate hearty. As they chowed down they specially enjoyed the stories Bronco told of when he cowboyed as a young man.

After the third day, however, Bronco began to slow down and lag behind in his efforts. He also began asking for a helping hand in most everything he did. Eden and his brothers kept throwing questioning glances at each other, but remained quiet on the subject. One morning, after breakfast, Bronco was left to himself. Eden, Boone, and Mason had ridden away to check on some horse stock grazing far out on the prairie.

Bronco started washing up the dishes then stopped suddenly, a thought consuming his mind. He began searching the shelves and cupboards of the kitchen. He even looked behind the cook stove. Nothing caught his interest until he opened the door to the walk-in pantry. It wasn't very big, but its shelves were stocked with plenty of canned good and sacks of flour, beans, and coffee; there were also small barrels of molasses, vinegar and sugar. He was about to close the door when a smile came to his whiskered face. On an upper shelf, behind a sack of potatoes, sat two fat bottles of whiskey. The glass sparkled like diamonds, and "bottle fever" hit Bronco hard.

Kicking off his boots, he made himself comfortable and leaned his chair back against the wall just outside the kitchen door. He gave a contented sigh and uncorked the first bottle. The sun was warming and the chill winds were fading. It didn't take Bronco long to get more than pickled, he got pie-eyed. Each sip of the reddish "coffin varnish" added to his radiant glow.

This job ain't so bad after all," Bronco muttered. "Matter of fact…"

Bronco suddenly turned his head in the direction of the big corral on hearing several horses whinny.

"Damn. Forgot to put out the hay."

Ignoring his boots, Bronco's bowed legs carried him and his bottle to the far side of the house and towards the corrals and barn.

"I'm comin'," he called, swaying noticeably to one side.

He climbed onto the corral, grabbing the top rail with both arms, leaving his right hand free to take another swallow from the bottle.

"Not feelin' much pain now," he muttered. "Praise the Lord."

The horses began prancing around the corral, anticipating their morning feed. But Bronco's bloodshot eyes focused on the blue roan standing off alone, ears back and nostrils snorting. Days earlier, Eden had cautioned Bronco about Old Gut Buster—the blue roan's well earned name. 'He's part bull and don't like red,' Eden had warned.

Bronco took another long swig of firewater and studied the horse closely. "I'm part bull myself," he mumbled.

Once the bottle was empty, and the man filled with liquid courage, he felt one hundred percent bull. It was no time at all before the blue roan was roped, blindfolded, and saddled. The horse hadn't made the slightest fuss either—which should have been a double warning right there.

"Old Gut Buster, huh?" said Bronco. "We'll just see whose gut gets busted."

Bronco swung into the saddle in one graceful move and made himself comfortable as if sitting in a rocking chair. Jerking the blindfold from the horse's eyes, Bronco was set for a wild ride. But the blue roan stood solid as a rock. Finally his head swung slowly to the left, and a round, glistening eye examined Bronco from his dusty sock to the top of his frayed hat.

"Ready when you are, knothead," said Bronco, pulled his hat down tight, and rammed his heels into the horse's flanks.

The blue roan began a slow walk across the corral, scattering the other horses, who wanted nothing to do with him.

Bronco began to chuckle softly. "Well, you ain't so…"

The blue roan dropped his head and exploded off the ground in the shape of a four-legged pyramid. He let out a frenzied, terrifying bawl, and did Bronco ascended towards the clouds.

When Eden and his brothers returned to the ranch, just before sunset, Bronco had already made his entrance through the Pearly Gates of Cowboy Heaven.

The funeral was short and sweet, but appropriate. Bronco was planted with his spurs and saddle, and a heart felt prayer.

Later, seated in front of the fireplace of snapping logs, the brothers were quiet and somber, and void of any appetite, since it meant eating their own cooking. But they couldn't get the idea out of their heads that they still needed a cook, a laundress, and…

"That's the answer," said Eden, half to himself, raising his head quickly.

"Answer to what?" asked Boone.

"We been goin' at this all wrong," replied Eden. "We need a woman."

"You're right," said Boone, sitting forward in his chair. "It takes a woman to do sweepin', washin' and cookin'."

"They have a knack for it for some reason," said Eden.

"They're born with it," added Mason. "Just like Ma. She could do anything."

"But how do we wrestle one all the way out here?" said Eden.

"What do you mean?" asked Boone.

"I doubt a woman would come clear out here to live with three men. Five countin' Chunk and Billy at the line shack."

"Least ways not a respectable woman," said Mason.

"He's got a point there," said Boone.

The three brothers slumped back in their chairs and stared into the fire.

"Got to figure a way through this," said Eden. "We'll die eatin' our own cookin'."

"And we need somebody that's goin' to stay permanent," said Boone. "Not like Dog and Bronco. I don't want anymore of that."

"So what do we do?" asked Mason.

"It sure would be nice to have a woman around the place," said Eden softly, then got up, crossed to the fireplace and leaned his hands on the mantle as he always did when deep in thought.

Boone and Mason knew Eden was right about having a woman about the place, but how to pull it off stumped them. So they each rolled a cigarette and pondered the problem in a haze of smoke.

Eden slapped the mantle with both hands and turned. He had a faraway look in his eyes as he collected his thoughts.

"What's goin' on in the nut of yours?" Boone asked.

Eden remained quiet, staring and planning.

"Must be good," said Mason. "He's thinkin' hard."

Finally Eden blinked, took a deep breath, and said, "One of us has to get married."

Stunned, Boone and Mason looked at each other, then Eden.

"That's sort of drastic, ain't it?" said Boone.

"Why get married?" said Mason, not liking the idea at all.

"Because it's the only way to get a decent woman out here," answered Eden. "And to make sure she stays."

"This situation is sure turning serious," said Boone, getting up and starting to pace around the parlor.

Mason just sat there rigid, puffy hard on his cigarette. "I'm sure we could find a woman to come out here without gettin' married."

"You know as much about women as a cat does," said Eden. "We have to do this right and respectable. No funny business."

"Ain't nothin' funny about this," said Boone. "But who's goin' to do it?"

"Simple," said Eden, and pointed at Mason.

"Me?" yelled Mason, jumping up and knocking his chair over. "When hell freezes over into a skating pond!"

"Now hold your potatoes," said Eden calmly. "You're the logical one."

"What logic?" replied Mason.

"You're the youngest, and best lookin' of the herd," said Eden.

"Eden's right," said Boone, relieved he hadn't been chosen.

"What about you two?" said Mason, defending himself as best he could.

"We're too old and set in our ways," said Eden.

"Right again," added Boone quickly. "No woman in her right mind would take up with us."

"You ain't old," said Mason. "Eden's only two years older than me, and you're only a year older."

"But you're still the best lookin'," said Boone.

"And what gal can resist a handsome young cowboy?" said Eden.

"It'll be as easy as sittin' in the shade eatin' a can of peaches," said Boone.

"You two are as crazed as a rabid skunk," said Mason, and stomped off towards the kitchen.

Eden and Boone stomped after him, determined to have their way. The sound of three pairs of agitated spurs filled the whole house.

Mason poured himself a cup of coffee from the pot on the cook stove and sat at the kitchen table. He refused to look at either of his brothers. Eden and Boone seated themselves gently across from him.

"All right,' said Eden after a few moments, "you don't want to do this, then how 'bout doin' all the cookin' and house chores from now on?"

"God help us," said Boone. "I'll get married before I go through that."

"Fine," said Mason. "Be my guest."

Boone ignored him and turned to Eden. "You know who'd make him a good wife? The widow Gibbon."

"What?" shouted Mason.

"And she's a hard worker, too," said Eden. "Does almost everybody's laundry in town, I hear."

"Saved every penny she's earned, they say," said Boone.

"And she's got enough kids to start her own school," said Mason.

"Right," said Boone disappointed. "Forgot that. She's got a wagonload alright."

"Well, she's out," said Eden. "Can't have a mob of kids runnin' around like Apaches on the warpath."

"I think one of you should get married," said Mason.

Eden and Boone sat staring at Mason, and he at them.

"You're right," said Eden finally.

"Hold on," said Boone, becoming uneasy.

"We'll do this far and square," said Eden, getting up.

Boone and Mason watched Eden cross to one of the kitchen shelves, pick something up and walk back. He slammed his hand on the table and took it away revealing a deck of cards.

"Low card does the marryin'," said Eden.

"Boone and Mason stared uneasily at the cards.

"Well?" said Eden. "We can't sit here all night."

"What do you have to say now?" asked Mason, taunting Boone.

Boone instantly took up the challenge. "I say I'm in."

The smile on Mason's face vanished and he stared at the cards again.

"Yellow as mustard, ain't you?" said Boone quietly.

"No, I ain't," replied Mason, sitting up straight.

"Well, what say you?" asked Eden.

"All right," said Mason, softly. "I'm in."

Eden spread the cards out in one long line, face down.

"Wait a minute," said Boone. "We all shake hands on this. That way nobody can back out." His last words were directed straight at Mason.

He and Mason shook hands roughly then shook with Eden. The brothers studied the worn cards carefully as if trying to divine which one was an ace. The crackling of burning wood inside the cook stove was the only sound to be heard.

Eden picked a card and threw it down. Queen of spades. Boone picked next. Ten of diamonds. Mason's hand shook as he took a card. Two of clubs. All the blood drained from his face and he looked kind of dizzy.

"That's that," said Boone, smiling.

"Yep," said Eden, sighing with relief. "Might as well turn in."

"I feel like that lamb in the Bible," said Mason.

"What lamb?" asked Eden.

"The sacrificial one," shouted Mason.

CHAPTER FIVE

The brothers were late getting away to town the next morning as they had to stop at the line shack to see Chunk Bascom and Billy Birdsong; the only cowboys kept on the payroll after the fall roundup.

"Don't worry about a thing," said Chunk, standing in the doorway of the old log shack. "We'll keep an eye on stuff."

"We gave the horses in the corral a good feed," said Eden as he and his brothers sat their horses, anxious to go.

Chunk was a tall, rough-looking man with a chest like a barrel, and legs and arms thick as logs. His hair and beard were as red as a Navajo blanket, and he spoke in a hard, gravelly voice.

"Figure on bein' gone two, three days, huh?" said Billy, squatting near a corner of the shack, rolling a cigarette.

"Don't know for sure," replied Eden. "Hope not. Could be longer."

"Billy was tall also; broad-shouldered, lean and wiry. His long, sleek black hair framed a deeply bronzed face. He wore all the trappings of an experienced cowboy, but he was a full-blooded Shoshoni Indian, and as handsome as they come.

"What's Mason so quiet for?" asked Chunk. "Looks a little peaked to boot."

"I'm fine," answered Mason gruffly.

"He just needs to get to town and unwind," said Boone, nudging Mason with his elbow.

"Got your sights set on some gal?" said Billy, grinning.

"Never you mind," said Mason, getting more irritated the longer he sat there.

"Better get ridin'," said Eden.

The brothers turned their horses and spurred them into a run.

"Kiss one of them gals for me," Billy called, and Chunk laughed loudly.

Once in town the brothers got themselves a room at the new Tellson hotel. While Mason scrubbed himself clean in a steaming hot tub, Eden and Boone rushed to the dry goods store and bought him a new set of clothes, along with boots, neckerchief, and a wide-brimmed hat. By late afternoon, Mason was clean as he could get, and dressed, brushed and polished from hat to spurs. He looked every inch the potential bridegroom, but felt he was going to his own hanging.

Eden and Boone sat leaning back in their chairs, feet up on a table, sipping whiskey. Mason stood before them for inspection.

"Now try and act civilized for a change," instructed Boone. "And mind your manners."

"You already told me that," snapped Mason.

"And smile," ordered Eden. "Women like a fella with a bit of a mischievous grin."

"And don't forget to brag about the ranch, and the cattle, and the horses," added Boone. "That way she won't think your tryin' to drag her off to some wolf hole out on the prairie."

"That's right," said Eden. "Ain't met a women yet wasn't interested in money."

Mason couldn't help staring at his brothers with hostile eyes. "I'm getting' tired of listenin' to you two."

Boone looked at Eden and shook his head. "He's got about as much sense as a cow in a stampede."

"Well, if you're so woman-wise," replied Mason, "where am I supposed to find all these wonderful females?"

"Already took care of that," said Eden. "While we was out we made inquiries."

"What sort of inquiries?" asked Mason, frowning.

"Eligible young ladies," said Boone with a wink.

"You just do what we tell you," said Eden, "and it'll all be over before you know it."

Fifteen minutes later, the brothers stood on the dusty wooden sidewalk outside Mrs. Hellfeather's boarding house. Oblivious to the town's activities around them the brothers eyed the large two story building with great interest. The entire place needed a fresh coat of paint and a new roof, but that didn't keep it from being a very busy establishment with boarders coming and going all hours of the day and night. A mob of children were whooping it up in the rear yard along with a mob of mongrel dogs of every stripe. The few women the brothers caught a glimpse of through the open windows, or lounging on the front veranda, were quite a bit older than what they had expected—especially Mason, who started to balk like a mule being driven into a small stall.

"I don't see nothin' here worth marryin', or even puttin' a saddle on," said Mason.

"Settle down," said Eden. "You got to start somewhere."

"Old Lum, down at the dry goods store, said Mrs. Hellfeather's daughter is a real looker," said Boone. "Ain't never been married neither."

"Must be somethin' wrong with her," replied Mason.

"Just go on in and look around," said Eden, losing his patience. "Her name's Viola."

"Pretend you're lookin' for a room," encouraged Boone.

Eden shoved Mason forward, sending him up the wooden walkway to the wide veranda. He couldn't help mumbling to himself the entire time. When he reached for the knob of the front door it sprang back and four young boys raced out, laughing and yelling, followed by an older girl with a fireplace poker in her tight fist. Her face was contorted in a snarl and all her teeth were showing.

"You make another mess in here," yelled the girl, waving the poker, "I'll bend this around your little necks!"

Mason wasn't sure if he shouldn't follow the boys down the steps as the girl turned her hostile eyes on him, along with the iron poker.

"Who are you?" she asked, snarling.

"I…uh…was…"

"What?" said the girl loudly.

"I was wonderin' about a room."

"Oh," replied the girl sweetly, and tossed the poker over her shoulder. "Step right in."

As Mason followed, he took a quick glance back to where Eden and Boone waited on the sidewalk. Both were motioning for him to get on with it.

The girl led Mason along a dark gloomy hallway towards the rear of the house. Loud voices could be heard coming from the second floor, along with stomping feet. On the main floor a baby was howling, and from the other rooms people could be heard laughing, sneezing, coughing and singing. The keys of an out-of-tune piano were being pounded on as if were a matter of life and death.

"Ma ain't here right now," said the girl. "But I can show you a room. Clean and quiet, too."

"Who were those boys?" asked Mason.

"Some rotten no-goods that live in the attic," replied the girl. "If they come back shoot 'em in the legs, will you?"

"Well, I…"

"Here's the room," said the girl, shoving open a worn, scarred door.

The room was small and windowless and crowded by a frail looking bed, one chair, one small table, and a battered dresser with a cracked mirror nailed against the peeling wallpaper. Mason entered and glanced around with a pained expression. He wouldn't have stabled his horse here. Then his eyes concentrated on the girl. He finally realized what a looker she was after she'd calmed down a bit. Her chestnut brown hair highlighted a prefect face as round and ivory as the moon. Her eyes were a sparkling sky-blue. She was a little shorter than Mason and filled out her bright red dress perfectly and tightly. And she had a smile attractive and inviting.

"Ain't seen you around before," said the girl, eyeing Mason closely.

Mason smiled back. He liked what he was looking at. "Would your name be Viola?"

"Yeah. How'd you know?"

"Oh, I told a fella I was lookin' for a place to stay and he said to come here. Ask for Viola."

She ran her eager, sky-blue eyes up one side of Mason and down the other before she spoke.

"So what do you think cowboy?"

"Well, is there somebody livin' in this room? I spotted a pile of clothes there under the bed."

"No. The room's vacant. Them's Rudy's clothes, but he don't need 'em. Got shot playin' poker last night. Like I said, you like what you see?" Viola came further into the room, closing the door partway. "I know I do."

Mason began to feel something was wrong, and grew uncomfortable. "I…I guess this would be all right. By the way, you…you married?"

"Why?" asked Viola, moving slowly towards Mason.

"Well, I…I…to be honest, I was lookin' for more than just a room."

"Like what?"

"A bride."

Viola was only inches from Mason when she stopped, stared a moment, then smiled.

"Why don't we pretend we're married already," said Viola, and flung herself against Mason.

They both fell backwards onto the bed and the brass frame shivered, and the bedsprings screeched. Mason was ready to do some screeching of his own as Viola crawled all over him, kissing and biting. For a few seconds he wasn't sure if he should stay or go.

The door of the room was thrown open, banging against the wall, shaking it, and there stood something out of a nightmare. She was four feet eleven inches tall, and almost as wide. The mound of white hair that was piled on top her head stood out in all directions like a basket of snakes. The faded dress and apron she wore was spotted with sweat and water. Her sleeves were rolled up past her elbows revealing strong, muscular arms of a hard working woman. Her expression was stone-like, but the sky-blue eyes were alive and fierce.

"Ma!" said Viola, sitting up quickly. "Done with the washin' so soon?"

"I told you I don't want to see no more of this carryin' on."

Viola jumped to her feet. "I was just showin' the room. He wants…"

"I know what he wants," snapped Ma, stomping further into the room in her oversized shoes.

Mason sprang off the bed and began backing towards the door as Ma circled in his direction, her meaty fists turning bright red.

"Your daughter's right," said Mason. "I was just lookin' for a room, is all."

"I'll give you a room in Hell," shouted Ma, grabbing the sagging wooden chair beside the sagging wooden table.

Mason turned quickly and proceeded down the hallway towards the front door, which looked miles away. His spurs were jingling in double-time. Ma and her menacing chair weren't far behind, though Viola was slowing her down somewhat by hanging onto one of the chair legs. Suddenly the leg popped loose and Viola went backward to the floor while Ma shot forward along the hallway.

Mason was almost to the front door when he made the mistake of stopping, and turning, to get in a final word.

"And I want you and your daughter to know," began Mason, "my mother taught me to respect women. And…"

"Well, she didn't teach you good enough," replied the rotund savage.

23

Mason only took two steps out the door before Ma's chair hissed through the air catching him in the back of the head. As he rolled across the veranda and down the steps, the front door slammed shut behind him.

Eden and Boone stood at the front gate of the broken down picket fence, dumfounded.

"He's got beans for brains," said Boone.

Eden simply shook his head slowly.

On the way back to their hotel, Eden and Boone pleaded with Mason to make one more try, but their words fell on deaf ears. Mason grumbled, rubbed the back of his head, and kept walking.

Inside the hotel lobby, Boone grabbed Mason by the arm and turned him around, stopping him.

"What do you do when you get throw'd off a horse?" said Boone. "You get right back on."

"You get back on," replied Mason. "I almost got my brain scrabbled."

"Hold on," said Eden, staring across the busy hotel lobby. "The answer's been right here the whole time."

Boone and Mason looked across the lobby, but didn't see anything to peak their interest.

"Exactly what you lookin' at?" said Boone.

"Right there," nodded Eden. "Through the fancy curtains."

Boone and Mason looked again, and saw the wide, curtained entrance to the busy dining room.

"What about it?" said Mason.

"Don't you see?" said Eden.

It was then Boone and Mason noticed four waitresses moving among the tables. They were dressed in snow-white, long-sleeved blouses and dark pleated shirts that reached to their ankles; and their silky hair was piled on top their heads in tight round swirls, and tied with bright colored ribbons. The women were all young, attractive, and smiling like angels.

"This is better than we hoped for," said Eden.

"You mean you want me to go and romance one of them waitresses, in front of everybody?" said Mason.

"Those people are too busy chowin' down to pay any attention to you," said Boone.

"And if those gals are good at waitin' tables," said Eden, "they could be good at cookin', too."

"Yeah," said Boone excited. "A waitress who can cook. A gift from God."

"How 'bout it?" said Eden to Mason. "One more try won't hurt."

Mason stared towards the dining room with a deep frown. "I don't know. I…" His mouth dropped open slightly, and he stared harder.

Eden and Boone looked back to the dining room and saw a tall, elegant young woman standing at the entrance, smiling and nodding to the customers who entered and exited. Her hands were clasped to her breast—angel-like—her hair was the color of dark mahogany; her green eyes shone like emeralds. But unlike the waitresses, her dress was satiny green and a ruby necklace and earrings completed her attire.

Mason couldn't help taking a few steps forward for a better look. "She's prettier than a painted wagon," he said softly.

Eden and Boone came up close behind him.

"Time to get back on that horse, cowboy," Eden said softly.

"Right," answered Mason, taking off his hat and smoothing his hair. "Just make sure she don't throw any chairs."

As Mason crossed the lobby, he couldn't take his eyes from this woman who looked more angel than human. He was determined to marry, no matter what.

The lovely vision nodded and smiled at two patrons as they left the dinning room, then turned her head to find Mason standing close, hat in hand.

"Good evening," she said in a soft, lilting voice. "I hope you enjoy your dinner."

"Mind if I ask your name, ma'am?"

"Hannah," she replied, smiling brightly.

"I'm…uh…Mason. Yeah, Mason McKenna."

"Pleasure to meet you, Mr. McKenna."

"I can't help saying this, and it's the truth, you're the prettiest woman I ever saw in all my life."

"Are you flirting, Mr. McKenna?"

"You must have a herd of men asking you to marry them."

"As a matter of fact, no."

"I can't believe it."

She looked down with sad eyes, saying, "I'm afraid it's true."

"What man wouldn't want to marry you?" said Mason, beginning to feel bolder.

"The right man just hasn't come along."

"Till now." Mason smiled and raised an eye brow. "I'm no saddle bum neither. My brothers and I own a big ranch."

"Is that supposed to be a proposal?"

"I sure want it to be. I've never done anything this loco, ever."

"Well, let me think," said Hannah, then smiled and nodded to two women entering the dining room. Turning back to Mason she replied, "I think you'd make a wonderful husband."

Mason's jaw dropped three inches. He looked over his shoulder to his brothers, who lounged near the wide front windows of the hotel, each smoking a cigarette and watching Mason's every move. He smiled at them and turned to Hannah.

"Then you'll…"

"Shall we get married now?" interrupted Hannah.

Mason could only stare. He couldn't believe this was happening. And so easy, too.

"What are you doing here?" asked a stern voice.

Mason and Hannah looked to the dining room entrance. A short, fat, bald headed man stood looking at them, eyes narrowed and angry. He wore a loud checkered suit and vest, and had a wide string tie knotted under his double chin.

"I told you there was going to be trouble if you kept coming back here," said the man.

"Now hold on," said Mason. "Who are you?"

"I'm the manager. And if you're with her, you can get out too."

"That's no way to talk to one of your waitresses," said Mason, his temper rising.

"She doesn't work here," snapped the manager. "And she's no waitresses either."

"I could be if I wanted to," replied Hannah, indignant. "But I wouldn't lower myself after this."

"Good," said the manager. "Get out. And I mean stay out."

"I've a good mind to let my husband, here, whip you like the dog you are."

"You're her husband?" said the manager.

"Well, I…"

"Yes, he is."

"Wait a …"

"Then take her home and tie her to a tree," said the manager.

"You swine," said Hannah, pulling herself up tall. She turned to Mason. "Let's go, Rodney, we're leaving."

"Rodney?" said Mason, confused.

Hannah stalked off across the lobby and out the front doors as the manager and Mason stood watching. Eden and Boone stared out the front windows as she passed.

"Who…who was that?" asked Mason.

"You're not her husband?" replied the manager.

"No."

"You must be new around here. That's crazy Hannah."

"Crazy?" said Mason loudly.

"She sneaks in here every once in a while, acting like she owns the hotel. One time she even tried to fire me. Can you believe that?"

The manager walked away leaving Mason staring into space with a dazed expression.

"What happened?" asked Eden, as he and Boone hurried up.

"How come she left?" added Boone.

Mason glared at his brothers, saying, "I get smashed in the head; now I almost married a crazy woman."

"She didn't look crazy," said Boone.

"Sure was pretty," said Eden. "Maybe she's only crazy once in a while."

"You two can chase yourselves up a tree," said Mason. "I'm done."

The rest of the evening was spent leaning against the highly polished bar of the Whiskey Barrel saloon—one foot on the brass rail and an elbow in the air. None of the three brothers were feeling any pain as Eden refilled their glasses from an almost empty whiskey bottle.

"If you'd a showed a little more grit and determination," began Boone, unsteady in his boots, "things would have turned out different."

"Why don't you take a walk somewhere," replied Mason in disgust, and swallowed his drink in one gulp.

"Let's not get discouraged," said Eden. "The night's not over."

"It is for me," said Mason, refilling his glass.

"He's backin' out," said Boone to Eden. "After shakin' hands on this."

"Well, I'd like to see you give it a try," said Mason.

"I could sure do better than some people I know," said Boone, and drained his glass.

"I think you could, too," said Eden.

"Damn right," added Boone.

"Well, go on then," insisted Mason.

"Don't want to," replied Boone, filling his glass.

"Say, Eden?" said Mason. "What color's the inside of a hardboiled egg?"

"Yella."

"Exactly," said Mason, staring at Boone with a smile.

"Now you're steppin' over the chalk line, cowboy," replied Boone, not liking Mason's insinuation.

"Yeah? Well, I think that tonsil varnish you're drinkin' is fillin' you with a lot of hot air."

"You do, do you?" said Boone, turning to face Mason.

"It's beginnin' to look that way, Boone," said Eden.

"Neither of you knows horse feathers about women," replied Boone.

"Then show us how it's done," said Mason, and gave a sweep of his hand towards the crowded saloon.

"All right," said Boone, slapping the bar, and putting his back to it.

His eyes began searching the smoke-filled, untamed room. There were plenty of painted women to choose from. All colors, sizes, and shapes—all pretty well worn to a frazzle. Boone was drunk, but not so drunk he couldn't see that he was letting himself in for trouble if he couldn't talk his way out. He turned back to the bar and poured another drink.

"Somethin' wrong?" asked Eden, enjoying Boone's predicament.

"Don't prod me," replied Boone.

"Yeah," said Mason casually, "you cut open a hardboiled egg and its all yella inside."

Boone drained his glass and slammed it on the bar. "Tell you what. Just to make this really interesting…" he stared down, rubbing his face, stalling for a way out.

"We're waitin'," said Eden.

"Stepped in a bear trap, didn't you?" said Mason.

"All right, all right," said Boone angrily. "First woman walks through them swingin' doors, I'll ask to get hitched."

"Them doors right there?" said Eden, pointing.

Boone gave a quick nod.

"I can't wait to see this," said Mason, grinning.

"Course I ain't standin' here all night for some…"

Boone was too dumbstruck to finish, and Eden and Mason couldn't believe what they saw either. Through the swinging doors came Dusty Sue.

Wide grins came to the faces of Eden and Mason, but Boone's face was pale and drawn.

Dusty Sue stood just inside the doors, studying the wildness and carousing going on. And she was dusty all right—just like always. She was a husky bear-like woman, dressed like a man, and with the eyes of a cautious cat. Her skin was leathery and creased as an old saddle. It wasn't because she was old; her life as a mule skinner for Caliban Freight was beginning to show on her considerably. In her gloved hands she clutched her long-barreled .45-70 rifle; and draped around her thick neck hung a well-used bullwhip.

Sue was about to elbow her way through the crowd when Boone appeared in front of her, escorted by Eden and Mason. Being several heads taller than the three brothers, Sue looked at them, and squinted hard, not sure what they were up to. Eden and Mason tipped their hats and retreated to the bar, leaving Boone stranded.

"What you lookin' at?" asked Sue. Her voice had a threatening tone.

Boone started to speak then stopped.

"You stupid or somethin'?" said Sue.

"I'm beginn' to think so," said Boone weakly.

"What?"

"Well, ma'am I..." Boone didn't have the nerve to go on.

"Spit it out, saddle bum, I'm dyin' of thirst standin' here."

"There's lots of women here," began Boon, "but I chose you."

Sue pushed her big dusty hat back on her matted, dusty hair and leaned in close to Boone. "You comparin' me to all them painted whores?"

"No," replied Boone quickly. "I meant I picked you to...to..." He shook his head, unable to continue.

"Picked me for what?" said Sue impatiently.

"To be my bride," Boone blurted.

Sue's eyes grew wild-looking and she burst out laughing. Boone glanced to Eden and Mason, leaning against the bar, watching then turned to Sue.

"Why in hell would I want to marry a cowboy?" said Sue, and laughed some more. "And a skinny one at that."

"Well, you ain't no prize heifer," said Boone, feeling insulted by her laughing.

Sue squinted hard, pushed her big hat back further on her head, and stepped closer.

Still leaning against the bar, Eden and Mason continued to watch. Though they couldn't hear what was being said, because of the noisy mob around them, and the stomping of boots, and rattle of whiskey bottles, they could tell things weren't going well. Sue kept poking Boone in the chest with her thick, gloved finger, and Boone was waving his hand in the air like he was herding cattle. That's when Sue hit him in the face with her large, knobby fist. Boone lay there staring up at the ceiling.

By the time Eden and Mason reached him, Sue was at the bar, glass in hand, and noisy as the rest of the drunks. The busy patrons didn't pay much attention to Boone, even when Eden and Mason carried him out the swinging doors.

CHAPTER SIX

Eden spent most of the next morning by himself; Boone and Mason staying in the hotel room to let last night's liquor wear off, and to lick their wounds. After wolfing down breakfast, Eden started for the livery stable to check on their horses, and give himself time to think more about this "marrying thing". It was starting to look like a good idea gone bad. But the sweet smell of a fall breeze, a powder-blue sky, and the warm white sun began to perk him up a notch. A young boy was lazily emptying buckets of water into a wooden trough at the corral of the livery as Stumpy Biggers, the owner, goaded him to work faster.

"I am workin' faster," whined the boy.

"I'll die of old age by the time you get that trough filled," grumbled Stumpy, and limped away on his one good leg.

Stumpy was a stoop-shouldered old man with no teeth and long white hair showing from under his battered and creased hat. His clothes didn't look much better, and he didn't smell any too sweet. But that was to be expected working at a livery stable seven days a week. Stumpy was headed for the huge barn when he spotted Eden approaching.

"Mornin', Eden," Stumpy called cheerfully.

"Mornin'."

"Headin' for the ranch?"

"Not just yet. Thought I'd check the horses."

"Still alive and kickin'," replied Stumpy, motioning to the corral.

Eden moved to the corral and a big gray horse with a thick black mane and tail trotted over. Eden ran his hands along the horse's neck and the animal nickered his appreciation.

"Where's Boone and Mason?" asked Stumpy, walking up.

"Still gettin' themselves pulled together."

"Did some drinkin' and womanizin', did you?" said Stumpy, eager to hear a good story.

"Guess you could call it that," said Eden then turned to Stumpy. A serious look came to his face. "You ever been married?"

Stumpy was stunned. "Why would I do that?"

"Never thought about it?"

31

"Nope. Never thought about shootin' myself in the head neither."

Eden was about to ask another question when he saw a tall, young woman emerge from the huge barn, pushing a wheelbarrow. Her face was red and sweaty, and her blonde hair was falling in her face; a few strands of straw stuck to her coarse gray dress here and there. She gave a glance towards Stumpy and Eden. Her dark blue eyes and flawless face cause Eden to stare harder.

She dumped the heavy wheelbarrow load of manure and straw beside the barn, turned and went back inside. A small pig was beside her watching her every move; staying close.

"Who was that?" asked Eden.

"Her? A prisoner."

"Prisoner?"

"Sheriff didn't want to keep her in the jail with all that assorted low life, so he brung her here. Fine with me. Can use some good help."

Stumpy looked to the young boy, who was still emptying buckets of water into the wooden trough.

"Good help's hard to come by," said Stumpy loudly.

"I'm workin' fast as I can," said the boy in a weary voice.

"Where does she stay?" Eden continued.

"Up there in the loft." Stumpy motioned to the barn. "I got her till she works off her fine."

"For what?"

"Well," began Stumpy, "the way it was told to me, she was stayin' at Mrs. Hellfeather's boardin' house; and seems two of the male occupants got liquored up and frisky, and got way out of line. The gal, there, says they forced themselves into her room, so she put the boot to them. Shoved one through a window, the other down a flight of stairs."

"I'll be damned," said Eden, grinning.

"That's what the two fellas said," replied Stumpy. "Unfortunately, for the gal, they was drinkin' companions of the sheriff and the judge, and she got thirty days for conduct unbecoming a lady."

The young woman came out of the barn with another wheelbarrow piled high with manure. Eden started towards her. But he wasn't sure exactly why. Stumpy paid no attention as he limped towards his helper at the trough.

"Them horses is goin' to die a thirst 'fore you finish," yelled Stumpy

The woman wiped the sweat from her face, grabbed the handles of the wheelbarrow then looked down at the little pig standing there, staring up.

"Will you quit followin' me. I ain't your mother," said the woman with a touch of anger.

The pig just wrinkled his nose and stared in anticipation.

"That animal harassin' you ma'am?"

The woman raised her head as Eden walked up, taking off his hat.

"He thinks we're related, I guess."

"Bit cool this mornin'."

"Not for me it ain't."

"Awful big barn to muck out by yourself."

"There's an extra shovel in there if you want it," said the woman, and started for the barn. Eden and the pig followed.

As the woman began shoveling, Eden seated himself on a small barrel and watched. Her dark blue eyes glanced at him several times as she worked, but she said nothing. Eden liked those eyes; the beauty in them; eyes unafraid and bold. He studied her thin, strong body; the body of someone who had obviously worked long and hard to make their way in the world. But most of all he liked her voice; it was low and eager and confident—almost audacious.

"Never saw anybody shovel manure before?" asked the woman.

Eden smiled. "Not that fast. You're good."

"I pride myself on my work," replied the woman in a sarcastic tone, and continued shoveling.

"How long you plan on stayin' around here?" asked Eden.

"Well, I'm not about to make this my life's work. I'm on my way west."

"This is the west."

"Ain't California," said the woman, stopping and mopping the sweat from her face with the sleeve of her dress.

"Headin' there to strike it rich, are you?" asked Eden

"That, and get married. I'm tired of bein' poor and alone."

"Sounds like you got your mind set good."

"A girl gets tired of searchin', waitin', and prayin'."

"Been doin' a lot of that, huh?"

"Years. Went to a matchmaker once. She came up with a bunch of scrub-uglies that would make that pig look good.

Eden looked at the pig. He looked back then concentrated on the woman, as if he knew they were talking about him.

"After that," continued the woman, "I tried being a mail order bride. Put ads in all those matrimonial magazines and newspapers."

"Any takers?"

"Sorry to say, yes. I went to Iowa once, Kansas once, and Missouri twice."

"And?"

"All liars. One was so poor he was lucky he owned a name. Another was already married…to a whiskey bottle. And the last two I gave a quick glance at and told them to kiss the back of my hand."

"Proud woman," said Eden, admiringly.

"Guess so. Can't feel sorry for ourselves. Cause then we lose our courage. And it's a sin to lose your courage."

"Amen. But California's a long ways off from here."

"Don't mind."

"Lots of men right around here might be lookin' to get hitched."

"Such as?"

"Me."

The woman stopped shoveling, glanced Eden up and down. Eden stood up and opened his coat so she could get a good look at him.

"Strong as a mustang and got all my teeth and hair," said Eden with a wink.

"I've seen worse."

"Thank you."

"But I hadn't planned on marryin' a saddle bum."

"And you shouldn't. You deserve better."

"And you're it?"

"Got a five thousand acre ranch, six thousand head of cattle, a hundred horses, and money in the bank."

The woman hesitated a moment, then said, "What kind of house you got?"

"Big. Lots of rooms, and weather tight."

"Keep it clean?"

It was Eden's turn to hesitate, then: "Most of the time."

"I'll believe it when I see it."

A surprised look came to Eden's face. "You…you mean…"

"I sure don't want to do this for thirty days," replied the woman, and threw the shovel down.

Eden stood there, unable to move or speak.

"Well?" said the woman. "You all talk?"

"I…I don't know your name."

"Minna. Minna Dunbar."

"Eden McKenna."

"Nice to meet you, Mr. McKenna."

"Same here, Miss Dunbar."

"Let's go," said Minna, grabbing a big, floppy hat from a peg on a post. "The smell's startin' to gag me."

As they left the barn Minna studied Eden some more.

"A cowboy, huh?" she said with a smile.

"Yes, ma'am."

"We'll see."

Eden noticed the pig walking along beside them. "What about him?"

"He can be the best man," replied Minna.

Things kept moving right along after that. Eden paid Minna's fine and court costs. Then he and Minna found the preacher. He was busy shoeing his horse and only stopped long enough to wipe the sweat from his eyes, roll down his sleeves, marry them, put the fee in his pocket, and go back to work.

"Man's all business, ain't he?" commented Eden as they walked away.

"No sense makin' this agonizing," said Minna.

"Guess we can go home now," said Eden shyly.

"Store first," said Minna.

Eden leaned against the long counter of Morton's Dry Goods and Mercantile Store, patiently rolling himself a cigarette, while Minna prowled the tables and shelves, picking out wedding presents to herself. There were shoes, dresses, hats; all colors of satin ribbons, long and short, for her hair, and fancy bedroom slippers and nightgowns. And aprons for the kitchen. The last of her plunder was a wide-brimmed hat and heavy wool coat for riding, along with a pair of fur-lined leather gloves.

"Want your wife to look pretty, don't you?" said Minna as she turned one way then another so Eden could get a good look at her in her new outfit.

"Pretty as a new-born colt," replied Eden.

With Minna mounted on a horse Eden had rented from the livery stable, they made a slow ride out of town. Minna's saddle, front and back, was hung with six sacks of goods she had chosen at the store.

They had just passed the hotel when Boone and Mason walked out the front doors. They buttoned their heavy coats against the cool morning wind, and glanced around the busy street.

"Wonder where Eden's got to?" said Boone.

Mason poked Boone with his elbow and pointed. Boone looked. Even though Eden's back was to him he recognized his hat, coat, and horse.

"Whose that with him?" said Mason.

The two squinted hard, and when Minna turned her head they saw her golden hair flash in the sunlight, along with a big smile. Boone and Mason glanced at one another, rushed into the middle of the street, and almost got run down by a stagecoach hurrying through town. The driver cursed them loud and long, but they paid no attention.

"Where'd he get that woman?" asked Mason as they stood enveloped in a large swirl of dust.

"Damned if I know," said Boone.

"You don't think he…" Mason stopped. He and Boone gave each other a questioning look.

"We better saddle up," said Boone.

The two of them turned and began running up the crowed street, spurs clanking.

Out on the prairie, the sun was at its peak in a cloudless sky, and the wind gently combed its way through the tall, darkening grass, moving it like waves on the sea.

Eden and Minna rode along leisurely, smiling and talking, testing one another; he to see what sort of woman she was; and her to see what sort of man he was. And the more they talked and tested one another, the more they began to think they'd made a pretty good bargain. And hoped the future would prove them right.

"Well, Mrs. McKenna," said Eden, "I sure hope you'll take to your new home. I'll do my best to please you, and make things enjoyable for you for a long time to come."

"And I'll do my best to do the same for you, Mr. McKenna. Marryin' is a leap in the dark anyway you look at it."

"Amen to that."

Out of the corner of her eye Minna saw something move in the distance. Staring, she said: "Wonder who that is?"

Eden squinted at the two dark objects. A slight grin came to his face. By the way the two riders sat their horses he knew it was Boone and Mason; following like two gun-shy coyotes.

"Too far away to tell," Eden finally said. "Well, if we're goin' to be home before dark, we'll have to make these horses sweat a little."

"Ready when you are," said Minna, getting comfortable in the saddle.

"Let's do it," said Eden, putting spurs to his mount.

Minna stayed right beside Eden as the horses eased into a gentle lope that took them deeper into the treeless prairie.

The nearer they got to the ranch, Minna began seeing grazing cattle everywhere. Black and white ones, brown and white; tan and reddish; all kinds of breeds; big and fat with horns longer than her arms. There were also scattered bands of horses moving lazily along as muscular looking colts ran frisky in the sun.

When Minna's eyes fell on the large log ranch house, her heart beat fast, and her face flushed. It looked like a palace to her as it spread out in the shape of a big T. The fireplace chimney of the parlor, and the tin chimneys of the wood stoves in the other sections of the house, reminded her of castle towers. Off to one side of the house were the corrals—big ones and small ones, like protecting walls.

The big bunkhouse and barn was impressive as the rest. Minna knew at once this wasn't a poor, broken-down cattle outfit. Her smile was as bright as he big blue eyes.

Eden opened the main door of the house and allowed Minna to go first. After a few steps she stopped in the middle of the wide parlor with its huge stone fireplace. Imitation oil paintings, of different kinds of wild flowers, hung on the walls. And there were curtains—beautiful embroidered curtains on all the windows. Minna saw instantly it was a woman's hand that had made the room so pretty and alive. She turned to Eden with that bright smile of hers. He smiled back, becoming more attracted to her the longer he looked.

"This was Ma's favorite room," said Eden.

"I can tell," replied Minna, and began looking around again.

"Better get a fire goin'," said Eden, "feels like it'll frost up tonight."

He moved to the fireplace and began building a fire. Minna walked to one end of the room, admiring the polished wood of the dark floor, the neatly arranged furniture, and the colorful hand-braided throw rugs. On the wall was a tin-type photograph of a tall, bearded man in a dark suit, standing beside a woman seated in a high-backed chair. She wore a plain dark dress and her gray hair was wound in a thick braid atop her head. The serious look of hard working pioneers was etched into the two sun-baked faces.

"This your Ma and Pa?" asked Minna.

"That's them," said Eden, kneeling at the fireplace as the kindling began snapping and crackling. "We sure miss 'em."

"We?" said Minna, turning to Eden.

Eden took a deep breath then looked up. "Well…you see there's…"

Eden was cut short as two horses came up fast to the house and stopped. Jingling spurs hurried towards the half open front door. Boone and Mason charged in, stopped when they saw Eden at the fireplace then took off their hats on seeing Minna.

Eden stood up, looked at his brothers, then Minna. He felt awkward under her questioning look.

"Boone, Mason," he said. "This is Minna. Minna, Boone and Mason.

"Ma'am," said the two brothers.

Minna nodded and waited for further explanation from Eden, but got none. She could see he was at a loss for words.

"And where you boys from?" Minna asked.

"Right here," replied Boone.

"We live here," added Mason.

Minna looked at Eden in surprise.

"I guess I forgot to mention I had two brothers," said Eden quickly.

"Yes, I think you did,' said Minna.

"Well?" said Boone to Eden. "Is she…you know…did you…"

Minna and I were married this mornin'," answered Eden.

"Damn," said Boone in surprise.

"I told you he went and did it," said Mason to Boone.

"Proud to have you in our home, Minna," said Boone.

"Kick off your boots and settle in," Mason added, smiling.

"Where exactly do you boys live?" asked Minna.

"Right back there," said Mason, pointing.

Minna threw Eden a quick glance and he looked away. All three brothers began to follow Minna as she began a closer inspection of the house. As she made her way down a long hallway she ran her fingers along the rough, peeled logs of the walls, stirring up quite a bit of dust. She gave a subdued cough.

"Little dusty," said Eden. "Winds been blowin' pretty steady out of the north."

"But you can fix that," said Mason.

"The wind?" said Minna.

"No, the dust," replied Mason.

Minna eyed him closely and moved on, the brothers' right behind. When she passed the open doors of the brothers' bedrooms she couldn't decide which room was the worst. The first looked like a barroom brawl had taken place; the second room a buffalo stampede; the third an Indian raid. To one side of each wood stove was a scattered pile of split firewood, and on the other side a metal bucket spilling over with wood ashes. Minna turned and looked at each of the brothers, studying them carefully. They smiled and waited for her to say something.

Minna walked on and found herself at the entrance to the large kitchen. It wasn't any better than the bedrooms. Containers of all kinds set open or on their sides on shelves, benches, and main table. A washtub full of dirty dishes, cups, knives, forks and spoons set on the floor beside the big cook stove, which had a spattering of grease, flour, and burnt molasses. There were several caste iron skillets to match the stove. The floor wasn't much cleaner, and the windows had what looked like smears of flapjack batter on them, but how it got their Minna didn't want to know.

"You boys should keep the kitchen door closed," said Minna. "That way the buffalo can't run in and out."

Eden and the others laughed, but stopped when they saw Minna was serious.

"We ain't much on cookin'," said Boone.

"But you can take care of that," said Mason in hopeful anticipation.

Minna ignored him and started across the kitchen, still not believing what she was seeing. Her foot hit something and a scorched coffee pot spun across the room ahead of her. But that wasn't what caused her to stop suddenly, and raise her eyebrows. In a far corner was a large pile of dirty, worn clothing—shirts, socks, long underwear, bandannas, assorted dusty, soiled vests and pants.

"We were gettin' ready to do the laundry," said Eden, "but we had to go to town. Right?" he added, looking to Boone and Mason.

"Was at the top of our list," said Boone.

"But now that you're here," said Mason, motioning to the soiled pile.

"That load'll take the kinks out of you,' said Boone, cheerfully.

Minna didn't appreciate Boone's attempt at cowboy humor and looked the three brothers over as if deciding which one to kill first. It was then they all heard a low growl; like a dog would make. The second growl was a bit louder.

"What is that?" Minna asked.

"My stomach," said Mason, apologetically.

"We ain't been eatin' too good lately," said Boone. "But now that you're…"

"I know," interrupted Minna. "Now that I'm here, I can take care of that, too."

"I'll bet you can cook up a storm," said Eden.

"Is that what you like to eat?" said Minna, sarcastically.

The brothers laughed, then grew serious.

"You…uh…can cook?" Eden asked cautiously.

The brothers waited anxiously for her reply, the tension showing in their eager faces.

Minna laughed softly and said, "You boys sure need help, don't you?"

"Like a steer stuck in a mud hole," replied Eden.

"All right," said Minna, "since I came this far I might as well…"

"What's that smell," said Mason, wrinkling up his nose.

Boone began sniffing the air. "Smells like horse manure."

Eden pretended he didn't smell anything.

"That'd be me," said Minna, a bit embarrassed.

Boone and Mason looked to Eden, who just shrugged.

"Guess I should wash up a little before supper," said Minna.

"I can do you better than that," said Eden. "Follow me."

Minna and the others followed Eden back down the hallway to a door at the far end. He motioned Minna on in with a big smile.

The bedroom was wide and well-furnished, and neat as a pin, like the parlor. A large double bed occupied most of the room, along with a small wood stove, dresser and mirror, and off to one side, a big brass bath tub.

"Ma was always proud of this big old tub," said Eden. "Came all the way from Saint Louie."

"It's beautiful," said Minna. "Must take a lot of water to fill it."

"Good as done," said Eden, and turned. "Mason you're elected."

"On it like a dog on a cat," replied Mason, as he hurried away.

"I better get the cook stove goin'," said Boone, heading for the kitchen. "Can boil a lot of water in a hurry on that."

"I'll get this one goin'," said Eden, walking to the small wood stove near the far wall.

He began tossing in kindling and wood shavings from a nearby brass kettle that also contained stove wood. "Have you fixed up in no time, Minna."

Minna sat on the edge of the big bed watching Eden build a fire then looked out the doorway to the kitchen, where Boone was busy getting a fire going in the cook stove—knocking over pots and pans in his rush.

"I'll be right in with the water," Minna heard a voice yell. She turned to the big window, on the other side of the bed, and saw Mason hurrying towards the well with two wooden buckets.

Minna smiled to herself, took off her gloves, coat and hat, and watched Eden blowing hard on the snapping kindling.

"You know," said Minna, "I got a feelin' there won't be many dull moments livin' around here."

"We'll try and keep it excitin' for you, Mrs. McKenna," replied Eden with a big smile.

"I'm sure you boys will."

While Minna was soaping herself clean as the proverbial whistle, Eden and his brothers made sure the cook stove was good and hot for cooking, and that the kitchen table was set in anticipation of a tasty meal. Their minds were more on what supper would be like that there being a naked woman in the house—and singing to herself as well.

As for the anticipated supper, the brothers were not disappointed. Minna more than lived up to expectations. Thick steaks and mounds of fired potatoes didn't last long, and neither did the beans with bacon and molasses. There were fist-sized sourdough biscuits with honey; canned tomatoes floating in vinegar, salt, and pepper. For dessert, spotted dog pudding—the rice boiled perfectly and seasoned with plenty of brown sugar, cinnamon, and raisins. The steaming cups of black coffee tasted better than the brothers had ever had in their lives.

To say they ate hardy is putting it mildly. A wolf would have had a hard time getting something off the table. Eden and his brothers used both hands; and Minna wasn't far behind them. In fact the brothers stopped for a few seconds to watch her stow it away.

"You sure like your own cookin'," said Boone, his mouth full.

Minna swallowed and replied, "When I was growin' up, we kids didn't get much but corn bread and bacon, so I admire good food when I can get it."

"Same here," said Eden, spooning a big gob of pudding into his mouth.

"We'll have to kill another steer tomorrow," said Mason, working on the last biscuit and honey.

"Good idea," mumbled Eden, chewing.

"First thing in the mornin'," added Boone, licking his spoon.

When the grub finally ran out everyone eased back in their chair and sighed contentedly.

"I'm double stuffed," said Boone, quietly.

"Feel like I died and went to heaven," said Eden, closing his eyes.

"Just like Ma used to make, I'm thinkin'," said Mason, wiping his mouth with his red bandanna, which was almost the size of a big napkin.

Minna, however, was still working on her spotted dog pudding and didn't take much notice of the compliments; she knew she was a good cook; nobody had to tell her.

"I'm happy you enjoyed yourselves," said Minna, her spoon scraping the inside of her bowl. "But the best is yet to come."

"I couldn't eat another drop," said Eden.

"Me neither," said Boone and Mason, shaking their heads.

"I don't mean now,"said Minna. "I mean breakfast."

"Deal me in," said Eden.

"I'll be there," said Boone.

"I'll have the stove fired up," added Mason.

"Now get on out and let me get the dishes washed," ordered Minna.

Eden and his brothers lost no time in fleeing from the kitchen chores. With their chairs pulled up close to the parlor fireplace, they smoked their cigarettes peacefully, and grew drowsy listening to Minna hum to herself in the kitchen. The brothers could barely keep their eyes open. Eden's head fell forward, and he jerked it back up, opening his eyes wide.

"Huh?" he said. "What'd you say?"

Boone roused himself. "I didn't say nothin'." He nudged Mason. "You say somethin'?"

Mason sat up straight, blinking his half-closed eyes. "No. Why?"

Eden tossed his cigarette into the fire. "Guess we better turn in."

Boone and Mason did the same and started to get up.

"That's right," said Boone, sitting back down. "Tonight's the weddin' night, ain't it?"

"I know," said Eden, starting to feel uncomfortable under the gaze of his brothers.

"Good thing you ate hearty," said Mason.

"Don't worry about my strength," said Eden testily, and stood up. "Go on to your stalls and bed down."

Boone and Mason walked away, smiling to one another.

Eden could see Minna was still washing dishes. He made sure his shirt was tucked neatly inside his pants and his vest straight. He smoothed his hair back and took a deep breath.

Minna was humming, and scrubbing a big iron skillet when Eden entered the kitchen. He stood watching her, not sure what to say.

Minna glanced at him, and kept scrubbing. "Where's Boone and Mason?"

"Turned in. We should too, I think."

"Just got a little more to do."

"That can wait. This is your weddin' day, you shouldn't be doin' no scrubbin' and cleanin'."

"Well, me and hard work are old friends."

Eden stood quiet, trying to figure out how to go on, since Minna wasn't being much help.

"How much longer you got there?" he finally said.

"Not long. You're probably tired, don't wait on me."

"I ain't tired at all. I'm used to being up late." Suddenly he stifled a long yawn with his hand.

"How's our room?" asked Minna without turning.

"All ready and waitin'," said Eden, perking up.

"Fire goin' good in the stove?"

"Forgot all about it," said Eden, looking in the direction of their bedroom. "Good thing you remembered."

"You better see to it, while I finish here," said Minna.

"Won't take but a minute." Eden started out of the kitchen then turned back. "Don't be long now."

"I'm practically there," replied Minna, rubbing the big skillet with a dry cloth.

Eden hurried to the bedroom and didn't take long in getting a fire blazing in the stove. He took a quick look around the disorganized shambles of the room and began straightening things here and there, finally getting the marriage bed in order. He fluffed up the thin, worn pillows to make them look better than they were; took several minutes to smooth out the sheet and blankets, making them neat and attractive. Not seeing anything else to occupy his time, he stripped down to his faded red long johns, pulled off his socks, turned the big kerosene lamp down low so the glow from the partly open door of the stove gave the room and intimate, cozy feeling. He got himself comfortable under the heavy blankets, folded his arms behind his head and stared at the bedroom door in blissful anticipation.

The longer Eden waited the sleepier he got. He was soon lying there eyes closed, mouth open, breathing loudly. The next thing he knew, Minna was easing gently onto her side of the bed. She was wearing one of the new nightgowns she had picked out that day, and her shiny blonde hair was all fixed up with bright blue ribbons. Eden smiled. Minna smiled back.

"Finally got here, huh?" said Eden, gently.

Minna nodded, gave a big yawn, closed her eyes, and pulled the blankets up over herself.

Eden hesitated a moment, then spoke. "You goin' to go to sleep?" he asked, a frown clouding his face.

"Been a long day," answered Minna, softly.

"Yeah, I know, but...we're here...on our weddin' night...in bed."

"And it's a lovely bed,' said Minna, only half listening. "Real soft."

"Well, we're legally husband and wife...and, uh...I figured...you know."

He began rubbing his hand gently along Minna's shoulders, then up and down her back. Minna opened one eye, watching his arm move. When it got to her rump her hand shot out like a rattlesnake, and slapped his hand away. Eden raised himself quickly on one elbow, an expression of shock and disappointment flushed his face.

"What's wrong? I thought..."

"Think again," said Minna, and closed her eyes.

Eden did think, but not for long. His hand began wandering up and down Minna's back again.

Again, Minna's hand shot out and slapped his hand away. Eden looked more confused and disappointed than ever. Minna threw the blankets off her and sat on the edge of the bed, looking over her shoulder at Eden. He waited, not sure what she was up to.

"I had a feelin' you'd start gettin' frisky," said Minna."

"Well, yeah," said Eden, upset. "You're my wife now and…"

"Yes, I am," interrupted Minna. "And I'll tell you when I'm ready. I ain't a brood mare, you know."

"No, but…"

Minna stood up, pulling a blanket and pillow with her, crossed to a long, pine bench against the wall, dragged it close to the wood stove, and lay down.

"Sleep tight, don't let the bedbugs bite," said Minna. "I'll keep the stove goin'. A bit chilly in here."

"I'll say," replied Eden, pulling his blankets tight around him. He began mumbling softly.

"You don't talk in your sleep do you?" asked Minna.

"Not till now," Eden shot back.

They both lay quiet, lost in thought, then Minna looked over at Eden, saying, "You don't snore do you? I couldn't stand much of that."

Eden made no reply and pulled the blankets up over his head.

CHAPTER SEVEN

Before sunrise, the next morning, Boone and Mason were busy in the kitchen. The cook stove was red-hot and you could hardly get near it without a wet blanket in front of you. A big pot of coffee set on top boiling and grumbling like a wild animal. As the brothers sat at the kitchen table with their cups of steaming coffee, they heard the door of Eden's bedroom slam shut, and the loud jingling of spurs as he came down the hallway.

"You really goin' to ask him?" whispered Mason.

"Why not?" replied Boone. "We're all grow'd men here."

"Mornin'," said Eden, gruffly, crossing to the stove and pouring himself a cup of coffee.

Boone and Mason watched closely as he came to the table and sat down. He stared into his cup. Mason looked at Boone and motioned towards Eden with a jerk of his head.

"Say," began Boone in a cheerful tone, "not to be nosy, but how did…"

"Mason," said Eden, "you finish shoeing them horses in the corral?"

"Two more to go," answered Mason.

"I want 'em all ready before the snow flies. We'll be doin' a lot of riding this winter to keep the herds from driftin' too far."

"Never mind that," said Boone. "How…"

"It's important," replied Eden, frowning.

"So's a lot of other stuff," continued Boone. "For instance, how was last night?"

"Last night?" said Eden, still frowning.

"Yeah, last night," said Mason, grinning.

"The honeymoon," added Boone, drawing the words out long and slow. "The bridal…"

"Never mind about my honeymoon," replied Eden, getting up and walking back to the stove.

Boone and Mason watched him pour more coffee into his cup, then stand there with his back to them. They looked at one another with raised eyebrows.

"Guess things didn't go accordin' to plan," said Boone, quietly.

"Wouldn't appear so," whispered Mason.

"What?" said Eden, turning to them.

"Nothin'," said Boone and Mason.

They all heard a door close, and Minna came down the hallway, humming. Eden walked to the far end of the kitchen table and sat down, still sulking.

Minna was rigged out in one of her new store-bought dresses, and her shiny blonde hair hung down over her shoulders, tied in two long horsetails by bright, red velvet ribbons. Boone and Mason where speechless, for a moment, because of how pretty she looked.

"Mornin', boys," said Minna, cheerfully.

"Mornin'," responded Boone and Mason, just as cheerful.

"Stove's good and hot, I see," said Minna, taking down a big iron skillet that hung on the wall.

"You can melt lead on it," cautioned Boone.

"But we'd rather have that great breakfast you promised," said Mason.

"Well, that was last night," replied Minna, turning to them. "I changed my mind."

"That's no big surprise," said Eden in a sour tone.

Minna, Boone, and Mason glanced at Eden, wondering what he meant, then continued their conversation.

"You mean no good chuck, like last night?" Mason asked.

"That was sure great chuck," said Boone.

"Oh, I'll feed you," replied Minna, dropping a spoonful of lard into the skillet; it began to sizzle and spit. "But after another look around, I can see I got my life's work ahead of me cleaning up this stable. So you'll have to swallow and get out."

"Fine," said Eden, getting up and stomping to the kitchen door. He quickly put his hat and coat on and went out.

"Is he always that soreheaded in the mornin'?" asked Minna.

"Not till recently," replied Boone.

He and Mason smiled at Minna, who shrugged and began fixing breakfast.

Despite the slight snag the newly weds had experienced, things moved along briskly at the McKenna ranch. The sunny fall days were crisp and bright, and everyone was hard at work. Eden and his brothers were gone most everyday, checking the horse stock, the herds of cattle scattered over the vast range land, and hauling in loads of logs to be sawed and split for firewood. The two hired hands, Chunk and Billy, were also kept busy, riding the miles of drift fence, getting it repaired before the winter storms began.

Minna was busy also, more than she had ever been in her life, but she never complained; she just kept on working and working—working and working. It started to feel like it was a twenty-four hour a day job, seven days a week. Cooking and cleaning. Washing and mending. Making all the beds. Then there was feeding the chickens, the horses in the corral, and one ornery mule that was only used when someone needed to take the buckboard to town for supplies. And there was milking to be done; luckily it was only one cow, but it was just as ornery and touchy as the mule, and Minna did more wrestling than milking.

Eden and his brothers were so involved in their day to day chores they weren't fully aware of Minna's unending labors, and how many little things there were that made up her day until well after sundown. Despite his long days, Eden still managed to get romantic every so often, but as tired as Minna was she threw cold water on that sort of conduct with a stinging slap, or the familiar words: "What do I look like, a brood mare?"

Eden was fast approaching the point where he'd kick his own dog, if he had one. But he never lost his respect or politeness towards Minna. However, he didn't know how much longer he could put up with this situation. As for Minna, she wasn't sure how much longer she could put up with doing a job meant for three women. It wasn't long before things came to a head. It happened on a Sunday morning.

Minna slouched in the kitchen doorway, watching Eden, his brothers, Chunk Bascom, and Billy Birdsong ride away to round up a large herd of McKenna horses that had strayed twenty miles to the north. Minna looked a little moody and irritable after having had to cook an extra large breakfast for five hungry wolves, instead of the usual three. The brothers had bragged on Minna's cooking so much Chunk and Billy wanted to get in on it, so Eden began having them ride in from the line shack every Sunday for breakfast. Well, Chunk and Billy weren't shy when it came to eating, and Minna had to juggle the hot skillets like never before to keep enough grub on the table so she could get some.

"Thank God, that's over," said Minna as she shuffled back into the kitchen, slamming the door behind her.

She began scrubbing and scraping pots, pans, and dishes like always, then after a while she felt guilty about how temperamental she'd been lately—sort of like the mule and the milk cow. She stopped scrubbing, realizing her attitude wasn't right; not in the least. She had a good home, good husband, fine brothers-in-law; life was better than she ever thought it would be.

"I'm not doin' right," said Minna. "I've got to change the way I'm thinkin'. Got to perk up, and right now."

Though the spirit is willing, sometimes the flesh grows weak. Which it soon did. But not until Minna had set into cleaning with a vengeance with broom, rags, and mop. The entire ranch house practically shined. She tackled the baking next—bread, biscuits, and pies were coming out of the oven as fast as she could roll the dough. While the bake goods were cooling, Minna fed the chickens and horses; milked the cow—after a short scuffle—and threw a rock at the mule when he tried to bite her.

Next, she had to face the chore she had been ignoring for a long as she could, then rolled up her sleeves—literally—and tackled the mountain of laundry. Not far from the kitchen door, she got a big kettle boiling above the hot coals of a big fire. Next to that stood a large kettle of cold water for rinsing, and a long bench where she rung out the clothes. The scrub board was beginning to take its toll. Minna's fingers and knuckles felt like they were getting worn down to the joints; her back and shoulders stiffened as she lugged bucket after bucket of water from the well. It took three rinsings to get all the soap out of everything. Then came the problem of where to hang stuff. It didn't take long for her to string ropes along the front of the bunkhouse, the ranch house, and clear across one of the small, empty corrals.

The horses, mule, and milk cow, in the bigger corral, were so fascinated with all the activity Minna was putting out they stood shoulder to shoulder staring through the rails at her.

Minna was just about finished with her Herculean task when she began to run out of steam. She stood between the bunkhouse and the ranch house with a heavy basket of wet laundry, wondering where to hang it all in the growing jungle of flapping shirts, pants, long johns, sheets, pillow cases, socks, and assorted vests. It looked as if a Fourth of July parade was marching by on both sides of her.

With sweat streaming down her face, and her hair, arms, and dress damp with soap and water, she decided a rest was in order. She moved sluggishly to the front porch of the ranch house, sat on the bottom step, rested her head on the edge of the wicker laundry basket, and closed her eyes. Slowly, she slumped to one side, her head resting amid the damp laundry. She didn't move or make a sound except for the deep breathing of welcomed sleep.

Towards sundown, Eden and his brothers came towards the ranch, their horses moving in an easy trot. Almost at once, they noticed there was no smoke coming from any chimneys of the house. Suddenly Mason pointed.

"Look," he shouted.

Eden and Boone now saw Minna sprawled on the steps of the front porch, her head still in the laundry basket. The brothers put spurs to their mounts and raced to the house. Dismounting quickly, Eden knelt beside Minna.

"Minna," he said, worried. "What's wrong?"

She revived somewhat, but was still groggy with sleep. She opened her eyes, slightly, and mumbled.

"What's she babblin' about?" Mason asked, concerned.

"She been drinkin'?" Boone inquired cautiously.

"No," replied Eden loudly then looked at Minna. "Least I don't think so." He took a quick smell of her breath. "Help me get her up."

Boone and Eden took Minna by the arms and helped her to a chair near the front door, and stood watching as she let out a giant yawn.

"She must not be gettin' any sleep," said Boone.

"Well, don't look at me," said Eden. "I ain't keepin' her up."

Minna's eyes and head finally cleared. She blinked as Eden came into focus.

"Oh, Eden, you're back."

"What happened?" asked Eden.

"Don't really remember," replied Minna. "I was doin' the wash and…"

"Looks like a Chinese laundry around here," interrupted Mason.

"Suddenly I felt kind of tired," continued Minna.

"Yeah, workin' a big ranch ain't easy," said Eden.

"You'll get used to it," said Boone, slapping her on the shoulder.

"Sure," added Mason. "Ma used to do twice what you're doin'."

"That what killed her?" mumbled Minna.

Eden and his brothers glanced at each other, not sure if they heard right.

"Listen," said Minna, pulling herself up straight, "I want to apologize for being so cranky lately." She looked at Eden. "And for some other things."

Eden grew slightly embarrassed. "No need to go into that now. You just set there and rest."

"Sure," said Boone, "you don't have to start cookin' right this minute."

Minna gave him a hard look, and was about to say something unkind, when she noticed the laundry basket lying on the steps.

"Oh, no, my laundry." She started to get up.

"Never mind," said Eden, shoving her back into the chair. "You rest. Come on, waddies, grab some clothes."

Eden and his brothers began wandering around with the basket of wet laundry, trying to find empty places to hang things, then started tossing the clothes on top the clothes already hanging.

As Minna watched, she began to recover her old self, and thought about all the work she had done since she came to the ranch and all the work yet to come—the days, weeks, and months yet to come. She wondered whether she would die at the cook stove or at the washtub, and neither prospect appealed to her. Suddenly her face brightened, her eye brows rose, and a smile came to her face. She had a plan.

"I should have thought of this sooner," she whispered. "What a lumphead. I know exactly what needs to be done."

As she sat thinking, and talking to herself, Eden and his brothers kept hanging laundry, and kept glancing towards Minna. They could see her lips moving, and noticed her nod her head every so often.

"She ain't losin' her mind all ready, is she?" Boone asked.

"Now what'll we do?" said Mason, worried.

"You two shut up," said Eden. "She's just fine."

"I'm not so sure," said Boone. "If this turns bad, you might have to get married again."

"That's right," agreed Mason.

Eden stared at his brothers in disbelief, threw a soggy pair of long johns in their faces, and walked away mumbling—just like Minna was doing.

Shortly after supper, that night, Boone and Mason saddled their best horses and headed for town for a little entertainment; and said they wouldn't be back till morning. They rode away howling like coyotes, their horses kicking up their heels.

Eden settled himself at the small roll top desk, on the far side of the parlor, and began going over the ledger book of the ranch, trying to decide on how many more head of cattle they could afford to buy next year; and whether to buy a few more thousand acres of range land, or just lease some government or Indian land. He kept rolling and smoking one cigarette after the other as he jotted down figures and notes to himself.

In the kitchen, Minna was hurriedly cleaning up the supper dishes, and glancing in Eden's direction every so often, like something important was on her mind. After everything was dried and put away, and the floor swept, Minna straightened her dress, looked at her reflection in the kitchen window and fingered her hair and ribbons just right, blew out the kerosene lamps, and walked towards the parlor, humming softly.

Eden, still busy figuring things in his head, didn't hear Minna cross to the fireplace where she added a few small logs to the fire. She looked at Eden, hesitated, then cleared her throat to get his attention. Eden looked over his shoulder.

"Minna," he said, smiling. "Didn't know you were there."

"Just finished up. Thought I'd turn in early for a change."

"All right. Goodnight."

Eden took the pen from the ink well and wrote something in the ledger. Minna took a few steps forward before she spoke.

"How…how's the stove in the bedroom?"

"Should be goin' good," replied Eden. "I put plenty of wood in earlier."

"Oh," said Minna, disappointed. She came closer, looked in the direction of the bedroom, then to Eden. "You sure the fire didn't go out?" she asked.

"It's fine," said Eden.

"Ain't you cold sittin' here?"

"Nope," said Eden, writing again.

Minna threw her hands up, walked to the hallway, leading to the bedrooms, and turned back. "Eden?" she said, sternly.

"Yeah?" said Eden, without turning.

"Eden, look at me."

Eden swiveled his chair around. Minna smiled and motioned with her head towards their bedroom. Eden leaned out of his chair and looked down the hallway, but didn't see anything out of the ordinary. "What?" he asked innocently.

Minna slumped against the wall and sighed. Eden wasn't making this easy for her. "God help me," she whispered.

"What?" Eden asked again, not sure what she had said.

"Do I have to draw you a picture?" said Minna.

"Of what?" said Eden, still puzzled by her attitude.

"What do you think," replied Minna, starting to lose patience. "Ain't we still on our honeymoon?"

"I didn't know we started one."

Minna stood up tall. "Never too late." She gave a wink and started down the hallway. "I'll be expectin' you."

Eden sat there, a moment then realized the honeymoon was on for real. He jumped up, started after her, then turned, blew out the kerosene lamp on the desk, and hurried across the parlor. He tripped several times, over his spurs, but managed to stay on his feet.

From that night on, a lot of tension that had been accumulating suddenly vanished.

Minna was happier in her work, and Eden was a new man. He and Minna were now truly husband and wife. They were completely taken with each other; cared about one another deeply. Though being married was new to them, the way they had started out was kind of turned around from normal—they both realized you were supposed to fall in love, first, then get married, second, but that just wasn't in the cards for them. Though they never said it to one another, they both wondered if this was love or something else. They didn't really know, but there was something forming between them, and it sure felt right, and full of peace. And if this wasn't love, well, it was sure to blossom sooner or later. These were feelings they'd never had before, and it required time, thinking, and some living.

Boone and Mason had to do some adjusting of their own with a woman in the house; had to watch their language—not that they hadn't when Ma was alive—but they sort of got careless with their words after she was gone. Gradually, they started shaving and combing their hair everyday; and didn't wear such smelly clothes anymore; and dusted themselves off before walking into the house. They were becoming gentlemen, of sorts. However, they still went to town several times a week to get the edge off, as they put it. At first they missed having Eden along, but reasoned those days were behind them, and so went on enjoying their own company.

Chunk Bascom, and Billy Birdsong fell in line quickly, also. Minna had insisted they start coming back for Sunday breakfast again. There wasn't any hesitation in their accepting, and their appetites hadn't changed a bit; they wolfed down everything in sight, practically. Chunk was extremely fond of gravy—great puddles of it on everything. Billy was partial to big biscuits hot out of the oven and right into his mouth. Once everybody thought they saw steam coming out his ears.

Minna's workload hadn't lightened up any, but things had lightened up in her mind. The plan she had crafted, the day she passed out doing laundry, was ever in her thoughts. And the plan was getting better and better as time went on. She just needed the appropriate opportunity to put it into action, one morning it entered on prancing horses.

Boone and Mason came riding in after a long, sleepless night carousing in town, but they were still bright-eyed and bushy tailed. When the two reined in at the big corral, Minna and Eden were there feeding the horses, mule, and milk cow.

"Well, I don't see a sheriff's posse followin'," said Eden. "You must not have got into too much trouble."

"Came close a few times," replied Mason.

"Not only did we have fun," said Boone, "we did some business, too."

"Like what?" Eden asked.

"Gettin' a jump on next springs cattle sale," said Mason, excited.

"Now, let me tell this," said Boone. "I'm the one run into the man."

"Were you drunk?" asked Eden.

"Not even close," said Boone.

"Was the cattle buyer drunk?" was Eden's second question.

"Sober as a judge," answered Boone. "Came all the way from Kansas City. Lookin' to talk to all the ranchers around here. I told him you'd be in to see him."

"He's stayin' at the Prairie Dog hotel," said Mason.

"I said let me tell this," ordered Boone.

"Well, tell it."

"I would if you'd shut up."

"Let's go see him right now," chimmed in Minna.

"That's what I say," said Mason.

"Now hold on," said Eden. "We usually sell all our stuff to the buyer from St. Louie."

"Well, he ain't here," said Boone. "And I'm sure Kansas City money is just as good as St. Louie money."

"I guess," said Eden, thinking.

"Let's all get cleaned up and go," said Minna, excited as Mason.

"I'm in," replied Boone.

"Same here," said Mason.

"You just came from town," said Eden, trying to settle everyone down.

"W can stand some more," replied Boone, smiling.

"We barely got started," added Mason.

"Guess it won't hurt to talk to him," said Eden. "Saddle up some fresh horses."

Boone and Mason leaped from their saddles and flung open the corral gate as Eden and Minna walked towards the house. Minna was all smiles. Her plan was coming together smoothly, and this trip to town was only the beginning.

CHAPTER EIGHT

Upon arriving in Sweet Water, Eden went to the Prairie Dog hotel to hunt up the cattle buyer from Kansas City, and everyone else went their separate ways—Boone and Mason to resume the mischief they'd started the night before; Minna proceeding quickly along the busy main street to the telegraph office.

Opening the front door, partway, she glanced around and saw the place was empty, except for the telegraph operator. He sat behind the counter, his back to the door, working the telegraph key with speed and precision, and talking to himself. He seemed to be having a very important conversation. Minna came to the counter and waited for the man to finish talking, and working the key. He sat back, looked up at the ceiling and rubbed his chin, continuing to mumble. Minna waited some more, then, when it looked like the man was never going to shut up, she tapped on the counter. The man jumped up and turned. A smile came to his long, pale horse-face. He was a frail looking old man with long, thin fingers. His big nose was long, and matched his face perfectly. A faded wool vest hung loosely on him, and the pockets were stuffed with short pencils and wrinkled wads of paper. His shirt and trousers were just as faded as the vest.

"Well, young lady, what can I do for you?" he asked in a slow, nasal tone.

"Need to send a telegram, quick."

"Sounds like an emergency. Something happen?"

"No, it's…just important is all."

"Well, then, have at it."

The man took a pencil and wad of wrinkled paper from one of his vest pockets and shoved them across the counter. Minna began slowly writing out her message. The man watched a moment, trying to get a look, then studied Minna closely.

"New in town, are you? Don't remember seeing you before." His eyes narrowed.

"Could say that," answered Minna, still writing. She then slid the paper and pencil back to the man. "How much?"

"Let's see." He held the message out in front of him and squinted. His lips moved with each word he read, then looked at Minna. "Don't want to include your last name?"

"First name's fine."

"Fifty cents should cover it."

The man leaned lazily on the counter as Minna took some coins from her coat pocket and counted them.

"Didn't I see you in church last Sunday?" asked the man.

"Don't think so."

"The name's Algernon Yates," said the man. "Please to meet you," he added, and extended his hand.

"Minna took it. "Minna McKenna."

"McKenna?" said Yates, straightening with surprise. "Eden McKenna's wife? I heard he got saddled and bridled. Never thought he'd…"

"Could you send that now?" interrupted Minna.

"Send what? Oh, the telegram. Get right on it."

Yates leaned on the counter again and scratched his chin. "How you like living out there? Must get mighty…"

"It's just like heaven," said Minna, losing patience. She slid the coins at Yates. "That should cover it."

"Get right on it," said Yates, starting to his desk, then stopped. "I almost bought some property out that way once, but…"

"How long before I get an answer back, you think?" said Minna, hoping to prod Yates to his desk.

He came back to the counter and leaned on it. "Glad you asked that. Can't never tell. Could be quick; could be late tonight; could be tomorrow morning."

"Tomorrow?" said Minna, worried.

"Things happen. The line could go down; the buffalo like to rub themselves against the poles; knock 'em over sometimes. Then there's the Injuns; jump the reservation, get liquored up, shoot the glass insulators off the top of the poles. They think it's fun, but…"

"I'll be back later," said Minna, walking towards the front door.

"I can have a boy bring you a reply. Just tell me where…"

"No, thank you," said Minna, going out.

Yates watched Minna hurry past the front windows, and scratched his chin. "Sure walks fast," he said to himself. "Don't do any good to get in a hurry." He turned and started to his desk. "Got to pace yourself."

On her way back to the Prairie Dog hotel, to find Eden, Minna's mind was racing. Her carefully laid plan had hit a snag. If the reply to the telegram wasn't in before she left town, she'd have to figure out a way of returning and retrieving the message without Eden and his brothers finding out. And she wasn't sure whether Algernon Yates would become a fly in the ointment or not. She was growing more worried by the minute.

"There she is now," said Eden, as he and Newton Miles, the cattle buyer from Kansas City, started across the hotel lobby.

Minna, head down, and trying to figure a way out of her predicament, moved away from the two men without noticing them. Miles looked at Eden questioningly. Eden gave an embarassed smile and waved his hat in the air.

"Minna," he called. "Over here, dear."

Minna turned, smiled slightly, and walked back, giving Newton Miles a quick study. He was shorter than Eden, dressed in a fancy dark suit, vest and bow tie. His boots were polished bright, and he held a derby hat in one hand and a large cigar in the other. His large gray eyes were as round as his head. Brown, thin hair lay smooth and flat like his long sideburns, and his cheeks were puffed out in a big smile. He was a prosperous looking man, no doubt about it.

Minna, meet Mr. Miles," said Eden.

"A pleasure, Mrs. McKenna," said Miles with a polite bow.

"Same here, Mr. Miles."

"Mr. Miles has made us a good offer on next year's beef herd," began Eden. "And I think we got ourselves a deal."

"I certainly hope so, Mr. McKenna," said Miles.

"But like I said, I got to discuss it with my brothers first."

"As you wish. Why don't you and Mrs. McKenna, and your brothers, join me for dinner tonight?"

"I was figurin' on headin' back to the ranch," said Eden.

"I hear there's going to be a big dance at the community hall," said Miles. "That could be a lot of fun."

Eden shrugged. "I don't know, I…"

"Mr. Miles is right," said Minna, eagerly. "It would be a lot of fun.

"Absolutely," added Miles.

"Well, I guess we could stay over," said Eden, still thinking about it.

"And that'll give us a chance to get better acquainted," said Miles.

"An excellent suggestion, Mr. Miles," said Minna.

Her plan had now become unsnagged.

The dinner at the hotel, and the big square dance at the community hall went off without a hitch; and though Minna and the others didn't get back to their hotel rooms till well after midnight, Minna was up at sunrise, getting dressed. She didn't know how early the telegraph office opened, but she was determined to be there when it did. She went out closing the door quietly, to keep from waking Eden, whose head was still buried in his pillow, and snoring softly.

The main street of Sweet Grass was beginning to come alive with freight wagons and mule skinners, buggies and buckboards; small herd of horses and steers were being hazed from one end of town to the other by whistling, shouting cowboys.

When Minna got closer to the telegraph office she saw a hand lettered sign in the window reading: OPEN. She flung the door wide, almost hitting Algernon Yates in the face as he swept the floor in a relaxed style that didn't raise much dust.

"Morning, Mrs. McKenna," he began in his tired, nasal drawl. "Looks like it's…"

"Anything?" asked Minna.

"Anything what?"

"A telegram; an answer to my telegram."

"Nothing yet," replied Yates, drawing the words out long and slow, as if needing time to think about it. "But like I said…"

"You sure you sent it to the right address?"

Yates eyed Minna with a touch of resentment. "If it's one thing I pride myself on it's…"

"I'll be back," said Minna, turning to the open door, then stopped. "No, I better wait."

"There's a comfy chair right there," said Yates, motioning to an armless, straight-backed wooden chair in a corner. "Won't cost you nothing neither." He laughed softly at his witticism.

"Thank you," said Minna, crossing to the chair. "That the right time?" she asked, looking at the large, loudly ticking clock on the far wall.

"Glad you asked that," replied Yates, leaning on his broom and staring at the clock.

In a few minutes, Minna's eyelids grew heavy as Yates began telling her the history of the large brass clock, and how it came to Sweet Water; and how it finally ended up on the wall. When Yates finished his long, boring story, he turned his eyes from the clock to Minna, and found she was gone.

He glanced around to make sure she wasn't wandering around the room, then shook his head.

"Sure is a nervous little heifer," he said softly.

Minna had only gone half a block when she saw Eden coming towards her. She forced a smile and waved.

"I been lookin' all over for you," said Eden.

"Just doin' a little sightseein', darlin'."

"You ready to have some breakfast?"

"Well, I…" Minna paused when she saw they were in front of the Sweet Grass Barber and Dental Emporium. "You look a sight," she said

"What?" said Eden, not understanding.

Minna grabbed him by the arm and pulled him through the open doors of the shop. "You need a shave and hair cut, you look like a goat."

"Wait a minute, I…" began Eden, but was cut short when the barber charged up, and patted him on the shoulder.

"Step right in, brother," said the barber with eager eyes. "You're my fist victim of the day."

Eden looked him up and down. He was big and bulky and needed a shave and hair cut himself; and the strong smell of whisky didn't make Eden feel very comfortable.

"Just funnin' with you," continued the bear-sized barber.

"To tell you the truth, I…" Eden started to say.

"Eden, sit," ordered Minna.

"All right," said Eden, hung up his hat, and dropped into the barber chair with a sigh of disgust. "But I need some breakfast before…"

"Don't you leave till you look like you're human again," said Minna, and walked out.

Eden sat forward quickly. "Well, where you goin'?"

The barber shoved Eden further back in the chair, and they watched Minns disappear into the milling crowd in the street.

"Soon as they marry you, they think they own you," said the barber.

"Who said we were married?" asked Eden.

"It's obvious," replied the barber.

Before Eden could reply, the barber tied a wide, soiled towel around his neck.

"Hair cut or tooth pulled?"

"A shave and…"

"The reason I asked, don't want to get confused and pull your hair and cut your teeth."

Eden stared at the barber, who stared back, then burst out laughing.

"Just funnin'," said the barber, slapping Eden hard on the chest. He took a swallow of whiskey from an open bottle on a shelf, near him, then began stropping his razor, wildly. Eden eyed him close.

When Minna made her second trip to the telegraph office she found Algernon Yates outside with a rag and bucket of water, cleaning the windows. A reply to her telegram had still not come. Wanting to avoid listening to Yates lecture on the correct way to wash dirty windows, Minna disappeared into a dust cloud the departing stage coach made, leaving Yates talking to himself.

With her stomach grumbling for breakfast, Minna kept wandering up and down the main street, watching carefully so as not to run into Eden, Boone or Mason, and have to return to the ranch. She had to have that reply to her telegram at all costs. But her luck wasn't holding. She came face to face with Eden again. He didn't look in a very good mood, and his hat set low on his head—almost to his eyebrows.

"I wish you'd stay in one spot," said Eden.

Minna didn't answer him. She studied both sides of his head then started to raise his hat, saying, "What happened to..."

Eden smashed his hat down lower on his head. "The man's a butcher, not a barber. I could do better blindfolded. If I hadn't run out of there I wouldn't have any hair at all."

"You didn't get a shave," scolded Minna.

"I didn't want my throat cut. You ready for breakfast?"

"Why don't you go get Boone and Mason, and I'll meet you back..."

"They already left for the ranch."

"Oh," said Minna, glancing around, desperate as to what to do next. Suddenly she smiled and grabbed Eden by the arm, leading him away.

"What now?" asked Eden as they walked three paces to the tall, wide windows of Kendall's Clothier Store.

"Did you notice the striking clothes Mr. Miles was wearing?" said Minna.

"He looked like a piano player in a whorehouse," replied Eden.

"There's just the suit for you," said Minna, pointing. "The suit of a successful rancher."

"Hold on, I ain't..."

Minna jerked him through the open door before he could finish.

Despite his protests, Eden found himself losing his hat, coat, vest, and gunbelt; and was forced to stand perfectly still while Minna eyed him from different angles, like she was about to paint his portrait.

Amos Kendall stood behind Minna eyeing Eden also, looking worried, and shaking his head; giving the impression that putting a suit on Eden was like putting silk pajamas on a pig.

"This could be a problem," said Kendall in a gloomy tone.

"What?" asked Minna.

"Look at him. He slouches, he leans. One knee goes that way, one this way. And one leg looks shorter than the other."

"My legs are the same, thankyou," said Eden, growing angry.

"Now, Eden," said Minna in a soothing voice, "let Mr. Kendall do his job."

"This could take a while," said Kendall, not sure he had anything to work with in Eden. "I'll need my measuring tape and pencil," added Kendall, and waddled away. "But I'm no miracle worker."

Mr. Kendall was a perfectionist, as his eyes bored into you or made a note with his pencil in a small ledger, he wouldn't be hurried. He was a short, rotund person with a shiny fat face, shiny bald head, and small, piercing dark eyes; eyes used to studying, measuring, fitting, creating a masterpiece in cloth.

"What'd you get me into?" Eden whispered to Minna.

"I just want my husband to look handsome and prosperous."

"I'll look like a half wit if I put on one of those things," said Eden, motioning to the suits of different styles and colors, hanging from wooden display racks like scarecrows.

"You'll look just fine," replied Minna, ignoring his protests.

After Mr. Kendall returned and began measuring and tugging here and there on Eden, Minna wandered casually to the front door; and casually looked down the street. She could just see a corner of the telegraph office, and nothing at all of Algernon Yates.

"Turn," ordered Kendall.

"Turn where?" replied Eden.

"Around. And put your arms out straight, if possible."

Eden turned his back to Kendall and swore softly.

"You always wear such noisy spurs?" Kendall asked with a frown.

"They go with my job," answered Eden, gruffly.

"A suit of quality doesn't need spurs."

"That's it," said Eden, and turned. "Minna, I..."
Minna was gone.

Crossing the wide, dusty street, Minna weaved in and out among people, freight wagons with their ox teams, buggies and buckboards, and riders on horseback. Her eyes, however, stayed fixed on the door of the telegraph office. When she tried to enter, the door wouldn't budge. She rattled the knob roughly; it still wouldn't open. She started to look through one of the windows when she saw a small sign leaning against the bottom, inside edge. BACK SOON, it read.

Minna let out a frustrated growl, and began looking around, wondering what to do. Not far down the street, she caught sight of a bushy crop of white hair moving among a crowd of people. The hair flopped up and down on both sides of a narrow head, like two chicken wings. It was Algernon Yates. Minna took off after him, dodging in and out among the hindering crowds. She was in the street one minute, back on the wooden sidewalk the next. She finally caught up with Yates and spun him around, stopping him.

"Where you goin'?" said Minna, breathlessly.

"Oh, there you are," replied Yates, relaxed as always.

"Why ain't you in your office?"

"Well, I can't deliver messages and be there, too," said Yates with great emphasis.

"A message for me?"

"Let's see." Yates reached into his vest pocket, bringing out a folded piece of paper. He squinted at it. "Got your name on it, all right."

Minna snatched the paper from him, unfolded it, and stared at it.

"I got to thinking you might be staying at one of the hotels," began Yates, in his smooth drawal, "so I figured I'd..."

He never got to finish. Minna threw her arms around him and gave him a big hug.

"Well, this is a pleasant surprise," said Yates with a wide grin.

"I'm goin' to bake you the biggest loaf of bread you ever saw," said Minna.

"I could go for some homemade bread, all right," began Yates. "My first wife used to make..."

He stopped when Minna whirled around and hurried away.

"That gal's going to wear herself down to a frazzle, moving like she does. Got to pace yourself."

CHAPTER NINE

After returning to the ranch, Eden had to stand up to considerable abuse from Boone and Mason; first, about his butchered hair, then about his new suit of clothes. Eden thought he'd pulled a fast one on Minna by buying a suit he saw lying on a display table, at Kendall's store, and not have to worry himself over a custom made one—that is till his brothers forced him to unwrap the bundle he had tucked under his arm. Boone and Mason showed no mercy about the "monkey suit", and how it had more checks and stripes than a horse blanket.

While Eden defended himself as best he could, Minna was in the kitchen fixing supper. She was all smiles and full of ideas. She didn't know much about babies, she thought to herself, but she couldn't let that hamper her any. Besides, she assumed Eden, Boone, and Mason probably knew even less; so Minna was determined to add a touch more to her overall plan.

When everyone was seated at the kitchen table, and eating with both hands as usual, Minna took a sip of coffee, cleared her throat, and sat ramrod straight.

"It always makes me happy to see you boys enjoyin' my cookin'."

Eden and his brothers grunted, nodded their appreciation, continued chewing, and reached for seconds.

"But," continued Minna with a sad face, "I'm afraid I might have to cut back some."

The brothers stopped eating, stared at Minna, then looked apprehensively at each other.

"I might have to cut back on a whole lot of things."

Eden and his brothers swallowed hard to get their food down, sensing what they were hearing didn't have good news attached to it.

"What...what seems to be bothering you?" asked Eden, carefully.

"We do somethin' to offend you?" Boone asked.

"We ain't used to being around women much," said Mason.

"Well..." said Minna, then paused.

Everyone waited tensely.

"We're all family here," continued Minna, "so I guess it's all right to just come out with it."

"What?" asked Eden, Boone, and Mason.

"I'm expectin'."

"Expectin' what?" replied Eden.

"A baby, lunkhead," said Minna.

Eden's jaw dropped noticeably. Boone's and Mason's eyes grew two sizes. Then all three brothers sprang to their feet like scared cats.

"Should we get a doctor?" Mason asked.

"Maybe you should lay down," Boone said.

"No, let's go back to town," Eden added.

"I ain't havin' it now," said Minna, trying to restore clam and reason. "I just brought it up 'cause we got to start thinkin' ahead."

"Right," said the brothers, and sat back down, their attention completely on Minna.

"Now," said Minna, relaxed and taking charge, "the way all this work has been goin' on around here, it needs a few alterations."

"Like what?" asked Eden.

"A lot of this hard work ain't good for the baby."

"Got a point there," said Boone.

"Need to cut down some, huh?" said Mason.

"Till after the baby comes," replied Minna. "And it would be a good idea for me to have some help."

"Good as done," said Eden. "Just tell us what our fair share is and…"

"That's sweet of you, Eden, but how would you boys be able to keep up with all you have to do, plus washin' and cleanin', cookin', and the other hundred things I have to do?"

"That's a good point," said Boone, eagerly. "We could be gettin' in over our heads."

"I agree," said Mason. "Especially if we have to do any cookin'. I'd rather eat barbed wire soup."

"But you said you needed help," added Eden.

"Yes, I do," replied Minna.

"We tried hiring some help a while back," began Eden, "and it went sour real quick."

"I'll say," said Boone, as Mason nodded in agreement.

"Some of these sourdough cooks can get touchy as a crazed rattlesnake," warned Eden.

"I'm talkin' about a woman's touch," said Minna. "And I'm sure your Ma would agree."

"A woman's touch?" said Eden, confused.

"We'll hire a girl from town. Someone who's perfect for the job," said Minna.

"Well…I guess that'd work," said Eden, glancing at his brothers.

"I like it," said Boone, relieved.

"That way we can concentrate on our own chores," said Mason, just as relieved.

"You let me handle this," said Minna. "Every time I go to town, I'll keep an eye peeled for just the perfect person. But just temporary help."

"Right," agreed Eden. "Just temporary."

"I like it," said Boone.

"We'll leave it to Minna," said Mason.

Everyone gave a smile of relief and went back to eating.

Minna began riding into town each week; staying all day, and returning to the ranch just before dark. Eden, Boone, and Mason were concerned about her doing so much riding, because of the baby, but Minna always put them at ease by telling them the baby was a long way off yet.

The brothers quizzed Minna on how the hunt for some temporary help was going. Again, Minna reassured them all was well; not to worry. She'd find just the right person sooner or later. The brothers smiled and agreed there was no hurry—didn't want any deadheads or troublemakers around to upset things.

What Eden and his brothers had no suspicion of was, Minna's ride to town every Saturday wasn't to look for help, but to check for any telegrams that would be coming in for her. It was a risky part of her plan, but it had to be done. Sometimes the telegram came early in the day, sometimes not till she was ready to start back to the ranch; but the message was always good. Not only that, Minna had become used to Algernon Yates's slow ways and endless speeches about whatever happened to pop into his head. While he rambled, Minna would simply look over his shoulder to the opposite wall, where a large calendar hung. She would count the days that had gone by, and the days to come, when her plan would reach its turning point. On her ride back to the ranch, she would tear up the telegram she had just gotten and the little pieces would scatter in the wind.

Finally, after the fourth week, and the fourth Saturday ride, Minna fixed her hair just right, using her best shiny ribbons; put on her best dress and shoes, and studied herself in the dresser mirror. Satisfied, she got into her heavy wool coat, put on her gloves and wide-brimmed hat, and sat anxiously outside the kitchen door.

The morning air was cold and frosty, as usual, with an endless, cloudless sky glowing lemon yellow on the horizon. Minna breathed deeply and smiled, but a frown came to her face when Mason came round the end of the house driving the ranch buckboard. He had hitched up Old Dirty, the mule, to it. His sinister looking eyes stared straight at Minna, and rumbling came from deep inside him as if he were softly laughing. Minna hadn't any love, or trust, for the ornery devil, and he felt the same about her.

"Why didn't you saddle one of the horses?" Minna asked.

"Eden and Boone took all the corral horses out to graze," replied Mason. "Won't have 'em back till late."

"All right," said Minna, softly.

Mason helped her onto the buckboard and handed her the reins. "When you're travelin' back," he said, "just give him his head and relax, he'll bring you here just like a homin' pigeon."

"From your mouth to God's ear," said Minna, still uneasy.

"Think you'll find somebody this trip?" asked Mason.

"I'm gettin' closer each time," replied Minna. "I think this could be it."

"Hope so. We worry you're doin' too much."

"Really?"

"Sure. Count of…you know."

"What?"

"The little one."

"Little one? Oh, the baby, right. I'll be showin' one of these days."

"Showin' what?"

Minna stared at Mason, a moment, gathered the reins, and said, "I'll explain later."

With a brisk slap of the long leather reins, Old Dirty headed out across the prairie in a strong trot, looking contended and gentle as a puppy; but his mule mind was working almost as fast as Minna's.

By the time Minna reached Sweet Grass, and traveled to the north end of town to the train deport, the sun was high, and the day growing warm. As Minna set the handbrake on the buckboard, wrapped the reins around one of the seat springs, she heard the faint wail of a train whistle. She hurried onto the wide platform of the depot and looked down the track. There was a dark spot in the distance with smoke trailing above it.

Minna took off her hat and gloves, turned to one of the depot windows, and studied her reflection. Her fingers brushed her hair one way then another, trying to get it just right, but a strong gust of wind rushed in twisting her long blonde hair, and ribbons, in three different directions. She stared at herself in the window, shrugged, and slammed her hat back on her head.

The train pulled in along side the depot platform, and came to a stop in a cloud of hissing steam, and clanging bell. The engine throbbed contentedly as passenger began appearing from the front and rear of the two passenger cars. The rest of the train consisted of a long baggage car, and a bright red and yellow caboose.

Minna waited anxiously, her eyes on everyone that came off the train, especially the women. After a few minutes the platform was deserted. A look of disappointment appeared on Minna's face. She crossed to the first passenger car and looked in one of the windows, but saw no one. When she turned to the next car, she saw two men stepping onto the platform. Each carried a large carpet bag and wore a loud checkered suit, vest, and a grey derby hat. On closer look, Minna noticed their suit coats and trousers were dirty, and had tears here and there. The derby hats looked as if they'd been beaten with an axe handle. The puffy, red faces of the two travelers had bruises on forehead, chin, and cheek.

The large door of the baggage car screeched open and the two rumpled travelers hurried towards it.

"Here we go," said one, loudly.

"I want satisfaction, now," said the other, angry and limping slightly.

Curious, Minna crossed to the far side of the depot platform to wait and see what was going on. The two men threw their carpet bags down and stared at the open door of the baggage car. Suddenly, from the dark interior, two scarred, leather suitcases, and two small, battered trunks were heaved out near the two men. Next came the conductor, a giant of a man with a look of exasperation clouding his sweaty face. Behind him came the baggage handler, a frail looking negro with white hair and sad eyes, and sweating just as profusely as the conductor.

The conductor look back into the baggage car, made an angry gesture, and said, "Come on, I don't have all day."

Two women appeared—the two Minna had been expecting, but not this way.

First came Leila, a slim young thing with reddish golden hair and dark green eyes, and what they called a peaches and cream complexion; one that would turn men's heads wherever she went. Her expression, however, was anything but alluring—it was closer to snarling. But she was dressed like a lady in a dark red dress, short black velvet jacket, high buttoned shoes, and delicate sunhat with long yellow ribbons dangling from the back.

Next came Narcissa with a bored, aloof attitude a mile wide. She was tall and dressed as if she'd just stepped center stage at the theater instead of onto a dusty train platform. Her long dress and wrap-around shawl, were of bright blue, her black hat narrow and bursting with fluffy white feathers. Around her swan-like neck was a wide black ribbon with a carved ivory brooch. Her long, curly black hair, brown eyes, and full lips gave an elegant aura to her marble-smooth skin. When she walked it was with the bearing of a royal personage. Her figure was, as they say, a feast for the eyes.

"All right," said one of the injured men, "what do you intend to do with these two?"

"I already done it," replied the conductor. "They're off my train." He turned to the women, saying, "And as long as you two breathe, don't ever set foot on my train again."

"That's right," added the negro baggage handler, shaking his finger. "You's givin' our train a bad name, 'cause you is…"

He stepped back quickly, tripping over his own feet as Leila took a menacing step towards him. The conductor blocked her way.

"Settle down, now," he said. "That's no way for a lady to act."

"Lady my eye," said the second injured man. "No lady smokes store-bought cigarettes."

"Cigarettes?" said the conductor, shocked.

"Both of 'em," said the first injured man.

The conductor's face turned a fiery red. "So you were smoking on my train, were you?"

"Never mind that," said the second man. "They assaulted us with intent to commit bodily harm. We want the sheriff."

"Well, go get him," replied the conductor. "I got more important things to do."

"We want to press charges," continued the man. "They could have killed us back there, shoving us off the train like that."

"We came back for you, didn't we?" said the conductor.

"And look at our clothes," said the other man, turning to show more tears in his coat and trousers.

"Well, you should have acted like gentlemen," said Leila, angrily.

"Gentlemen?" said the other man. "I'll have you know we're from Texas, and…"

"That explains it," interrupted Narcissa, her eyebrow raised.

"What's that supposed to mean?" the man growled.

"Women don't act like this in Texas," added the other man.

"Well, you're in Wyoming now, so get used to it," replied Leila.

"May we go now?" asked Narcissa in a bored tone.

"With pleasure," said the conductor.

"No," yelled the two men.

Suddenly, Minna swept into the center of the group, all smiles, acting like nothing was wrong.

"There you are," she said, taking the women's suitcases. "Sorry I'm late, let's go."

Leila and Narcissa each grabbed a small trunk, and dragged them along the platform, following Minna.

"Good riddance," said the conductor, and started back into the baggage car.

"To bad rubbish," added the old baggage handler.

"Aren't you going to stop them?" asked one of the men.

"No," yelled the conductor, without turning.

Minna, Leila, and Narcissa hurried down the steps of the depot platform to the buckboard. Minna and Leila quickly loaded, and tied, the luggage to the rear rails, while Narcissa reached into her small, velvet handbag and took out matches and a cigarette.

"What did you two get into?" asked Minna in a harsh whisper.

"They started it," replied Leila.

"Started what?" asked Minna.

"We made the mistake of being nice, and talking to the two ninnies," said Narcissa, blowing a long stream of cigarette smoke into the air.

"When did you start that?" Minna pointed to the cigarette.

"It's all the rage in Chicago," replied Narcissa. "Buy them already made."

"She's been acting like the Queen of Sheba since we started out here," said Leila. "I been dragging her luggage all over the place for her."

"You know I have weak wrists," said Narcissa.

"I notice you don't have any trouble eating," replied Leila.

Narcissa ignored her and puffed away.

"Why'd you shove those two off the train?" Minna asked.

Narcissa motioned to Leila, saying, "Because Miss Brawler, here, got carried away."

"I wasn't about to let nobody play patty fingers with my behind," said Leila.

"They did?" said Minna, surprised.

"Leila and I were getting some fresh air on the rear platform of our car," began Narcissa, "when the two ninnies appeared to continue the conversation we'd started with them inside."

"They weren't interested in conversation, I can tell you that," said Leila to Minna.

"I could have handled it," said Narcissa, "if you would have remained calm; instead of acting like the heavy weight champion of the world."

Minna had to laugh, and so did Leila.

"Before I knew it," continued Narcissa, "both of them were flat on their backs in the dirt, and all I could do was wave goodbye."

"Sounds to me they got what they deserved," said Minna.

"That's what I said," replied Leila.

"Don't you three go nowhere," said a male voice.

Minna, Leila, and Narcissa turned and saw one of the injured men limping down the steps of the depot platform.

"My associate is on his way to get the sheriff," continued the man, "so don't you move a hair."

The three women glanced at each other, unintimidated.

"Let's go," said Minna.

Minna and Narcissa climbed onto the seat of the buckboard, while Leila made herself as comfortable as she could among the luggage.

"Oh, no," said the man, limping forward, grabbing the long leather reins resting on Old Dirty's rump.

"Drop those reins," ordered Minna, "or you're goin' to be limpin' permanently."

"Really? And how's that going to happen?" said the man.

It was then Old Dirty swung his head around. His big lips seemed to form a slight smile, and he bit the back of the man's leg, hard. The man howled and staggered away. Minna drove off with Old Dirty hee-hawing in deep satisfaction.

The sun was low in the sky, and great patches of white clouds were drifting lazily to the south. The late afternoon breeze was growing cool as the buckboard appeared at the top of a slight rise in the limitless sea of grass. Old Dirty plodded along sleepy-eyed, his ears slanted back as if listening to the conversation of the three women.

"Well, you two don't seem any worse for wear after all this time," said Minna.

"Been close to three years since we seen each other," said Leila.

"How much further is it?" Narcissa asked

"Not far," replied Minna.

"And where is everybody?" said Narcissa.

"I like it," said Leila, looking around excitedly.

"Well, I'm hungry, and my rump's sore," said Narcissa in an irritated tone. "We been on stage coaches, trains, more stages coaches, then more trains. I need a long, hot bath and a quiet room."

"You're not goin' to a hotel," replied Minna. "It's a ranch."

"Is it fun, Minna?" Leila asked eagerly.

"Hell no. I'm being worked to death. But that gave me the idea to send for you two."

"Why?" asked Narcissa, lighting another cigarette. "So we can join you in your misery?"

"You've both been yappin' for years you can't find the right kind of fellas," said Minna. "So I decided to help you out. How many of those things are you goin' to smoke," added Minna, staring at Narcissa's cigarette.

"I relaxes me," said Narcissa. "Just keep driving."

"I can't believe you got married," said Leila.

"Neither can I," replied Minna. "But suddenly there I was, there he was, and the time seemed right. That's the only way I can explain it for now."

"What do these brothers look like?" Narcissa asked. "The wrath of God, I suppose?"

"Just wait," said Minna, "you'll be surprised."

"I get the cutest one," said Leila.

"Anything that wears pants is cute to you," said Narcissa, taking a puff on her cigarette.

"Look who's talking," Leila snapped.

"Now remember," began Minna, "I hired you to help out at the ranch. And you've hired out lots of times, so you're used to all kinds of work."

"Exactly what is this kind of work?" Narcissa asked with a frown.

"I'll explain when we get there," said Minna.

"And we're supposed to help out till the baby comes, right?" said Leila.

"That's part of the plan," replied Minna.

"Have you thought up a name for the little bastard?" asked Narcissa.

"I said I was married, didn't I?" said Minna, loudly.

"I hope it's a little girl," said Leila, "then we can dress her up in all kinds of pretty dresses and little shoes, and lots of bows and…"

"Don't rush me," interrupted Minna, "we got other things to do first. Now when we get there…"

The buckboard came to an abrupt stop, and Minna and the others were jerked forward. Old Dirty looked back, eyed the women, and sat down and closed his eyes.

"What the hell's he doing?" asked Narcissa.

"What's it look like?" said Minna.

"Is he tired?" inquired Leila, innocently.

"How do I know?" replied Minna, and began slapping the long reins hard.

Old Dirty didn't pay the slightest attention. He opened his mouth once, like he was yawning. Minna slapped the reins harder. Old Dirty flicked his tail.

"Well, isn't this wonderful," said Narcissa. "I came all this way to sit here and starve; or be butchered by Indians."

"Then think of somethin'," said Minna in disgust.

Narcissa took a quick look around then pointed. "Leila get me that rock."

"Why don't you get it?" replied Leila.

"I have my good shoes on."

"Well, what do you think I got…"

"Hurry up," ordered Narcissa.

Grumbling to herself, Leila climbed down, picked up a fist-sized rock, and handed it to Narcissa, who flung her cigarette away and stood up. She studied the back of Old Dirty's head, spit on the rock, and threw it. Old Dirty never twitched an ear.

"Well, that was almost a good idea," said Leila, sarcastically.

"Leila," said Minna, "kick him in the ribs."

"I don't want to get near him," replied Leila. "You saw what he did to that fella back at the depot."

"Just kick him and jump back," said Minna.

Leila stared at Old Dirty, then move forward, cautiously, saying, "If I get bit I'm…"

"Just do it," said Minna, impatiently.

"She's always whining about something," said Narcissa.

Leila hesitated, kicked as hard as she could, and jumped back. Old Dirty sat there like a stone statue.

"He ain't got a nerve in his body," said Leila.

"We'll see about that," said Narcissa, taking a long pin from the right side of her hat.

"That ought to do it," said Minna, smiling.

Narcissa held the pin out to Leila. "Here. Stick him good."

"You trying to get me killed?" said Leila.

"You're right," said Minna to Narcissa, "she does whine a lot."

"Don't get me started," replied Narcissa, rolling her eyes.

Leila stood there with the long pin in her hand, studying Old Dirty.

"We can always walk the last ten miles to the ranch," goaded Minna.

"If we're not eaten by wolves," added Narcissa.

Leila eased up to the mule's rump, and got herself set to stick him. Minna and Narcissa waited patiently. Leila gave a quick jab and jumped back. No reaction at all from Old Dirty.

"You better make sure he's not dead," said Narcissa.

As quick as a cat, Old Dirty was on his feet and running. Leila barely managed to grab onto the rear of the buckboard as it went flashing by. While Minna was frantically sawing on the reins in an attempt to control the mule, Narcissa was busy clutching the seat of the buckboard with one hand, and her hat with the other, and cursing a blue streak that would have made a teamster blush.

Leila, screaming, clung precariously from the rear of the buckboard with both hands as she was dragged along, grass and dust flying up on both sides of her. After losing one of her shoes, she managed to pull herself to safety, and flop down onto the luggage, where she joined Narcissa in a loud display of colorful language.

Old Dirty was making good time in his dash for the ranch, and there was nothing anyone could do to stop him.

Half a mile ahead, at the summit of a small hill, appeared Boone and Mason, driving a herd of thirty horses back to home range. Off to their right they could just make out the shape of Billy Birdsong, on horseback, also bringing in some stray horses. As the brothers started down the hill they heard shouting and looked further out onto the prairie. They recognized Old Dirty and the buckboard, and realized both were moving at an unusually fast pace.

"That Minna I hear yellin'?" Mason asked.

"Can't tell," replied Boone. "But somethin' ain't right."

"Never saw Old Dirty move that fast before," said Mason.

"He must have lost his mind," said Boone. "Let's go."

The two brothers put spurs to their mounts and raced down the hill towards the buckboard. Billy Birdsong had also seen what was happening and joined in the chase from his direction.

Despite the weight of the buckboard, and the three women and luggage, Old Dirty had hardly worked up a light sweat, and hadn't slowed down for a second. He seemed to be enjoying the situation. But the same couldn't be said for the women. Minna was leaning back with all her strength on the reins. Narcissa still had a death grip on the seat of the buckboard and her wildly waving feather hat. Leila had both arms wrapped tightly around one of the small trunks. The faces of the women were grim with determination, and their voices strong with unkind words concerning Old Dirty's heritage. He must have understood most of it because when he came to Little Tongue Creek, he tore right down the center of it with a vengeance. The creek was only ankle-deep, but it was wide and wet. The wheels of the bouncing buckboard sprayed tall rooster tails of water onto the women in an endless stream.

Sensing he wasn't far from the ranch, Old Dirty left the creek bed, anxious for a good feed of hay and oats. Then he saw Boone and Mason riding towards him. He must have thought they wanted to race because he did a quick turn, and charged back down the middle of the creek.

Minna, Narcissa, and Leila had given up trying to control the situation and just sat there, silent, while they had their second bath of the day.

Billy Birdsong came riding in close now, giving a wild war whoop in hopes of making Old Dirty turn out of the creek. He did; never slowing his pace, and swung the heavy buckboard in a complete circle causing grass and dust to fly skyward. Leila was the first to be tossed out, along with the two suitcases and the two trunks. Next was Minna, then Narcissa, both rolling through the tall grass like they were playing some sort of kid's game. Then, Old Dirty stopped as suddenly as he had started. He blew loudly through his wide nostrils, snorted contentedly, and eyed the women flopping in the grass. He sat on his rump, nodded his head, and brayed loudly,

Seconds later, Boone, Mason, and Billy rode up and jumped from their horses.

"Minna, you all right," asked Boone, helping her to her feet.

Minna's wide-brimmed hat was mashed tight over her eyes, and she was a bit shaken up.

"That you, Eden?" she gasped.

"No, Boone."

Mason was getting Narcissa to her feet, trying to be as helpful as possible, but couldn't keep a smile from his face as he glanced her up and down. The feathers of her drenched hat hung over her face, and her dripping dress clung to her like a soggy blanket.

"Easy, little sister," said Billy, trying to steady Leila as she swayed back and forth. "Any bones broken?"

"What?" said Leila, flipping the torn brim of her waterlogged hat up out of her eyes. She staggered a few steps with Billy following, hands out, ready to catch her if she fell.

"Give me your gun," yelled Minna to Boone. "I'm goin' to kill that mule."

"And I'll help you," yelled Narcissa.

"No, you can't kill Old Dirty," said Boone, keeping his hand on his revolver, so Minna couldn't get it. "He's like one of the family."

"Not my family," shouted Minna.

"Or mine either," added Leila, staggering up beside Narcissa.

Boone stared at Leila and Narcissa, completely puzzled, then leaned in close to Minna.

"Who are these women?" he asked softly.

"Oh, I forgot," said Minna, pushing her wet hat back off her forehead. "This is Leila and Narcissa."

Boone, Mason, and Billy quickly removed their hats and nodded politely. There was an awkward pause as the men and women stood looking at each other.

"Exactly where were you goin'?" Boone finally asked.

"To the ranch," replied Minna. "Before that knothead spawn of Satan…"

"Looks like he gave you a good ride, all right," said Mason, still suppressing a grin.

"Give me your gun," said Minna, thrusting out her hand.

"Now settle down," said Mason.

Boone leaned in close to Minna again, and spoke softly. "But why are they goin' to the ranch?"

"I hired them. Finally found some good help. Now collect up their luggage, please, and put it back in the buckboard."

"Sure thing," said Mason.

Mason, Billy, and Boone collected the scattered suitcases and trunks, and placed them quickly in the rear of the buckboard. Leila couldn't take her eyes of Billy, tall and handsome as he was, and with that long shiny hair and deep, dark eyes.

"Thank you," said Leila sweetly, and smiled as Billy moved past with her suitcase.

Minna grabbed Leila by the sleeve and gave her a quick jerk, saying, "Quit that."

"What?" said Leila, innocently.

"You know what," replied Minna.

"All set," said Boone, slapping one of the trunks he had tied in place. "Best head back before it gets dark."

"I'm not riding in that thing again," said Narcissa, motioning to the buckboard.

"That makes two of us," said Leila.

"I don't blame you," said Minna. "Boone you let Narcissa ride with you, and Mason you take Leila."

"Well, I…" Boone hesitated, and looked at Mason, wondering if that was the proper thing to do.

"And Billy," continued Minna, "latch onto that knothead. I don't want another bath."

"Yes, ma'am," replied Billy.

The ride back to the ranch was slow and quiet for a little while. Billy rode close beside Old Dirty, holding tight to his headstall. Minna sat thinking all sorts of nasty thoughts concerning mules in general. Boone and Mason rode stiff in their saddles, stone-faced. Narcissa and Leila, however, were enjoying themselves despite the drenching they'd had, and rode comfortably behind their man, holding on tight.

"I hear your ranch is quite something," said Narcissa, sweetly.

"Yes, ma'am. It's…it sure is," replied Boone, feeling ill at ease with Narcissa's arms around his waist.

"I think I'm going to like it there," said Narcissa, tilting her head to one side, giving Boone a wide smile.

Red-faced, Boone gave a quick, nervous smile back, and swallowed hard. "Didn't figure on Minna hiring two helpers," he said, awkwardly.

"The more the merrier as they say," replied Narcissa. "Will you teach me to ride?"

"Well, I…I guess I…"

"Ride like the wind. I read that in a book once. Ride like the wind. But I guess I already did that. Only I didn't figure on getting drowned."

"No, ma'am."

Leila had a bear-hug hold on Mason, and he kept glancing back out of the corner of his eye at her, like he was enjoying it.

"Mason," said Leila, softly to herself.

"Yes, ma'am?"

"Oh, I was just saying your name. I like it; sounds romantic."

"It does?"

"Absolutely. Real romantic. And you did rescue me."

"Well…guess…so."

"Is it much farther to the ranch?"

"Couple more…"

"My butt's getting tired."

Mason had no reply to that, and just stared straight ahead.

The sun was starting to set, and a strong wind swept in off the darkening prairie when Minna and the others rode up to the kitchen door of the ranch house. Eden stood there, mouth open, and staring at the three bedraggled women. It took him a few minutes to recognize Minna then rush to the buckboard to help her down.

"What happened?" he asked.

"I'll explain after I pull myself back together," said Minna.

"Old Dirty acted up a little on the way back," said Boone.

"A little?" said Minna, loudly. Then to Eden, "We're goin' to have to have a talk about why we need a mule around the place."

"But he's just like one of…" began Eden.

"I know," said Minna. "Like one of the family. Well, so am I."

Eden turned his attention to Narcissa and Leila as Boone and Mason helped them from their horses. Billy had dismounted and was unloading the suitcases and trunks from the buckboard. He couldn't keep from grinning; Narcissa and Leila reminded him of two witches he'd seen in a play once in Grand Forks, the night the new theater opened.

"I see you brought some company with you," Eden said to Minna.

"More than that. They're my new helpers. Narcissa and Leila."

The two women gave an embarrassed smile, and fussed nervously with their long, stringy hair, trying to make themselves presentable.

"You hired two?" said Eden, frowning slightly.

"Two for the price of one," said Minna, proudly. "Right, ladies?"

Narcissa grudgingly gave a quick nod, and Leila gave a polite, "Yes, ma'am."

Eden shrugged, saying, "If you need 'em, then…"

"I figured they could stay in your Ma and Pa's room till we get the bunkhouse fixed up."

Narcissa and Leila looked at each other, not liking the idea of being hustled off to a drafty old bunkhouse.

"I think you women folk better get dried out and into some clean duds," said Boone. "Before you catch pneumonia."

"That's right," said Eden, and motioned towards the kitchen door.

"Come on, ladies," said Minna, "let's wring ourselves out."

Eden escorted the women inside, and Boone and Mason picked up the luggage and followed. Billy swung up onto his horse and led Old Dirty towards the barn.

"Let's go, mule, before you get yourself hanged."

Old Dirty nodded his big, bony head and nickered contentedly.

CHAPTER TEN

Early the next morning the wind eased in off the deep prairie, bringing with it the frosty feel of deepening autumn. The sun crept lazily upward as if reluctant to share its warmth.

Eden and his brothers were already at work in one of the small corrals behind the barn.

Eden and Boone were on foot swinging their long ropes, waiting for Billy Birdsong, on horseback, to haze a string of twenty horses towards the center of the corral. Eden and Boone quickly dabbed their lassos around the heads of two skittish mustangs as they plunged by, trying to dodge the flying loops. The two horses then stood quiet and gentle. Mason, with sleeves rolled up, and a heavy leather apron hanging from his waist approached them. With a pair of long-handled nippers, he began clipping off the bent ends of the horseshoe nails that held the iron shoes on the solid hoofs.

"Billy," Eden called out, "once we get this bunch unshod, run 'em out and bring in some more."

"Ain't I goin' to get a breathin' spell here?" asked Mason, his nippers clicking rapidly.

"Hell, you haven't even worked up a sweat yet," said Boone, smiling.

"I want half our saddle stock runnin' barefoot before winter sets in," added Eden. "It'll be good for 'em."

Narcissa stood near a corner of the ranch house watching Eden and the others working the horses. Minna and Leila were a few yards behind her, splitting and stacking firewood. The three women were in plain wool work dresses and short, heavy coats, and their wide felt hats were held securely to their heads with long scarves ties under their chins. The gusts of wind blew hard every so often, warning them that fall was quickly passing.

"Narcissa," said Minna, wiping sweat from her forehead, and lowering her heavy axe, "what are you standin' there for?"

"Just looking," replied Narcissa without turning, her eyes on Boone.

"I told you she thinks she's the Queen of Sheba," said Leila, and tossed an armload of split wood onto a pile at the side of the house.

Narcissa finally turned. "That Boone is quite the handsome one."

"He can't hold a candle to Mason," replied Leila.

"Who asked you?" said Narcissa, taking a cigarette and matches out of her coat pocket.

"I told you they were a good catch," said Minna.

"They sure don't pay much attention to us," said Narcissa.

"Put some bait out and reel them in," replied Minna.

"I agree with Narcissa," said Leila. "They only seem to notice us is when we have food in our hand."

"Give 'em time," said Minna. "You haven't been here that long."

"Long enough to become your slaves," said Leila, tossing another armload of wood onto the pile.

"That reminds me," said Narcissa, puffing on her cigarette. "When are we going to be paid?"

"After you do some work," said Minna.

Narcissa motioned to the growing mound of firewood. "And this isn't?"

"You ain't seen nothin' yet," replied Minna.

"You mean there's more?" asked Narcissa.

Minna chuckled to herself and began spitting more wood.

Leila sat down on the wood pile and let out a tired sigh. "I'm feeling discouraged. I didn't come all this way not to get married. I want a big house and big garden. And two, maybe three, kids. How many you having, Minna?"

Minna stopped chopping, glanced at Leila, embarrassed, and shrugged.

"What about you, Narcissa?" Leila asked.

"A house, yes," replied Narcissa, walking towards them. "But I'll have to think about the brats. I don't know if I could stand all that screaming and whining."

"Well, I'm all for you girls gettin' hitched quick, too," said Minna. "Eden's a handful all by himself. And the faster you marry, the lighter my chores'll be around here."

"How sweet are you on Eden?" Leila asked.

"Well," said MInna, thinking, "Eden's a fine man, a gentle man. And he's certainly provided a good home here. Better than any other I've had."

"But do you love him?" Narcissa asked.

Minna smiled. "I'm workin' on it."

"Does he love you?" said Leila.

Minna thought a moment then looked towards the corral. "I sure hope so."

"Let's get back to us," said Narcissa, taking a puff on her cigarette, and seating herself beside Leila.

"Yeah, right," said Leila with a nod.

"I think you should get things moving," said Narcissa to Minna.

"Me? I don't want to marry those two. They're all yours."

"Yes," said Narcissa, "but it wouldn't be lady-like for us to go pouncing on them like a couple of house cats."

"Not lady-like at all," added Leila.

"It's the man who should do the pursuing," said Narcissa.

"Right, again," said Leila.

"At least we have to let them think they're doing the pursuing," continued Narcissa.

"Oh, I like that," said Leila.

"So you're dumpin' all this in my lap?" said Minna.

"It was your idea from the beginning," replied Narcissa.

"Besides," said Leila, "we're going to get on each others nerves if we keep working together."

"A very good point," said Minna. She looked towards the corral, thinking. "I better see what I can do."

Late that afternoon, Boone was busy inspecting, and greasing, the windmill that stood like a lonely sentinel five miles out from the ranch house. There were cows milling around the long, wooden water trough beside the windmill, and herds of other cattle were scattered across the prairie as far as you could see. Some of the mother cows, nuzzling their calves, suddenly threw their heads up and stared suspiciously at an approaching rider. It was Minna, riding a long-legged buckskin mare. It trotted gracefully through the tall grass, shaking its thick black mane and tail, feeling confident and frisky in the warm afternoon sun. The pungent fragrance of wild sage filled the nostrils of horse and rider, and Minna was feeling confident and frisky herself.

As she rode towards the windmill, and the unsuspecting Boone, his horse stopped cropping grass and looked up, giving a long whinny. Boone, from the top of the windmill, saw Minna rein in.

"What you doin' way out here?" Boone asked, smiling.

"Just takin' a ride," replied Minna, dismounting. "Sure a beautiful day."

"Enjoy it, 'cause when winter comes, it'll come a roarin'."

Minna began climbing up the ladder towards Boone.

"Careful now," warned Boone. "Hang on tight."

When Minna reached the platform of the windmill she remained on the ladder, the wind whipping at her hat and heavy coat. Boone had the big fan of the windmill facing out of the wind, and held securely with two heavy chains.

Minna grinned as she looked Boone up and down. He was streaked with dark grease—hat, face, arms, shirt, and pants.

"You got more grease on you than the windmill," said Minna.

"I know," said Boone in disgust. "It's embarrassin' to have to do sodbuster work. I wouldn't mind so much if I could do this from the back of my horse."

Minna nodded and grew serious. "Yeah, every once in a while you need a helpin' hand. Like me. That Narcissa and Leila are a God send. Couldn't ask for better help."

"Well, I'm glad they're workin' out for you."

"Kind of cute too, ain't they?"

Boone had to think a moment. "Yeah, guess they are. Sure look better than when I first saw 'em."

Minna and Boone laughed.

"Looked like a couple of drowned rats," said Minna.

"And then some," added Boone.

"But I think Narcissa's kind of lonely; being way out here and all."

"Think so?"

"Yep. She's always wantin' to talk, wantin' company. She sure is a fine worker."

"Glad to hear it."

"And a good cook, too."

"I noticed that," said Boone with a little more interest.

"That apple pie last night was one of hers," said Minna.

"That was worth shootin' somebody over."

"She's makin' another one for tonight."

"I'll be first one to the table."

"Just between you and me," began Minna, as if she didn't want anyone to hear, "I think she's got her eye on you."

"Why? What'd I do?"

Minna stared at Boone, a moment, wondering if she were wasting her time.

"I just meant, I think she's gettin' interested."

"In what?"

"In you," yelled Minna.

Boone shrank back slightly, a bit shocked at the out burst.

"I'm sorry," said Minna, forcing a smile. "I think my foot slipped." She glanced down. "Nope, I'm fine."

She motioned for Boone to come closer, and he leaned in.

"It wouldn't hurt if you talked to Narcissa now and then," said Minna. "Make her feel at home. Like she's part of the family."

"Sure…okay. I'll keep it in mind."

"Wonderful," said Minna, a bit discouraged. "By the way, where's Eden and Mason gone off to?"

"Eden rode over to the line shack to see Chunk and Billy; Mason's about two miles out that way, checking fence line."

"Well, you be careful up here," said Minna. "Don't want to break your neck and miss out on Narcissa's apple pie."

"Now that would be a tragedy," replied Boone.

After Minna climbed down, she mounted her horse, waved goodbye, and drifted casually as possible, in the direction Boone had indicated Mason was working. She felt she hadn't had much luck getting Boone headed in Narcissa's direction, but was determined to do better herding Mason to Leila.

Singing softly to himself, Mason spliced a section of broken barbed wire in a lower strand of fence line that ran for miles east and west. His horse stood a short distance from him, sleepy-eyed and whisking its tail to drive away the flies. A distant whinny caught Mason's attention and he looked quickly over his shoulder. Minna came galloping towards him, waving her hat.

"Minna," yelled Mason, waving back. "You lost?"

"Just ridin'," replied Minna as she reined in. She looked down the long fence line, saying, "Looks like you got a day's ride ahead of you."

"Oh, I should be done before sunset."

"Don't be late for supper. Leila and Narcissa are so happy being here, they're cookin' up somethin' special for tonight."

"That so?" said Mason, his interest peaked.

"Those two are a God send," said Minna.

"Workin' out fine, huh?"

"Couple of angels. Specially that Leila."

"She did seem kind of spunky."

"Oh, you noticed, did you?"

"Seems like a real nice gal."

Minna shrugged. "Yeah, but I think she's lonely, or homesick."

"That's too bad."

"You know you're her age, maybe you could kind of give her a little attention. Make her feel welcome. You two could have a lot of fun together, I bet."

"Guess I could do that," replied Mason, rolling the thought around in his head.

"Good," said Minna, encouraged.

"Course I got a lot of chores to do first," added Mason, and went back to mending the fence. "Winter's comin'."

"Yeah," said Minna, slightly discourged now. "That's what I keep hearin'. But Leila won't be here forever. Soon as the baby comes, she's gone."

"Well, you be sure to let them two do most of the chores," said Mason, mounting his horse. "I know he don't show it, but Eden's proud as punch about that baby."

Minna forced a smile. "Well, I'm proud as punch about the baby, too."

"Pick a name for the little critter?"

"Uh…no. I'm still thinkin'."

"Got to be ridin', said Mason. "See you at sundown."

Mason rode on along the fence line, whistling softly. Minna slumped in her saddle and gave an anxious sigh.

"God Almighty," said Minna, quietly. "This is like pullin' teeth."

With the darkness came the full moon, and the howling of wolves gathering for a hunt. Their bold chorus faded in the long hiss of wind sweeping through the endless grass.

Eden, wearing a brand new pair of red long johns, jammed more chunks of firewood into the glowing bedroom stove, then lay down on his side of the bed and watched Minna. She stood at the dresser mirror brushing her long silky hair. Her thin nightgown outlined her tall, graceful body in the delicate glow of the kerosene lamp. Eden smiled.

"You sure are a pretty woman, Minna McKenna."

"Thank you, Eden," replied Minna, turning and studying his smooth, freshly shaven face. "You're a handsome husband."

"You always look pretty."

"Even when I get dragged behind a mule?"

Eden laughed. "Even then."

As Minna continued brushing her hair, Eden kept gazing at her, half dreaming about what their future would be like.

"You should be startin' to show one of these days," Eden said, gently.

Minna stared at his reflection in the mirror, then realized what he was referring to.

"Gosh, yes. I can hardly wait."

Minna set her hair brush down, and lay across the foot of the bed, and studied Eden again. "I been thinkin' a lot about our marriage lately."

"Me, too," said Eden.

"I think everybody should get married."

"Nothin' wrong with that."

"Take Boone and Mason; seems all they do is work, work, work."

"That's mostly what cowboyin' is," replied Eden.

"And Narcissa and Leila; they work, work, work."

"That's what you hired them for."

"Yeah, as long as you give 'em a prod once in a while."

"Lazy are they?"

"No. I think they just turn their minds to other things?"

"What things?"

"Boone and Mason."

"Really?"

"Have they mentioned anything about the girls to you?"

"Not as I can remember."

"You're brothers ain't gettin' any younger, you know. One of these days they'll be two old men strugglin' to saddle their horses."

"Never thought much on that," said Eden, rubbing his chin.

"Well, Boone and Mason should. And I think Narcissa and Leila would fit right in."

"Just what are you gettin' at?"

"Narcissa and Leila are mighty interested in your brothers."

"You sure?"

"Postive. And I think we should help things along."

Eden began rubbing his chin again, thinking. "I don't know if we should get in the middle of anything like that. Maybe you should just let things take its course, and…"

"Nope. Ain't got time for that."

"I'm not so sure Boone and Mason are thinkin' along the same lines as you."

"Then convince them."

"But…"

"You like being married, don't you?"

"Of course."

"Then Boone and Mason will, too."

"I…"

"As your wife, I think you should support me in this."

"Well…" said Eden, hesitantly. "I can't make any promises about Boone and Mason; they're grow'd men, you know, and…"

"That's no problem," said Minna with a wave of her hand. "You got married, they should get married."

"Maybe you're right. If I had to, they…"

"Had to?"

"I meant…not had to…I meant…"

"Never mind, we'll talk about that later."

Minna got up and began brushing her hair, and humming softly. Eden stared into space, wondering what he had gotten himself into.

CHAPTER ELEVEN

Two days later, with Narcissa and Leila still prodding Minna to keep things moving concerning Boone and Mason, Minna began prodding Eden to quit stalling and get things moving with Boone and Mason. Eden resigned himself to treading across shaky, unknown ground, in hopes that Minna would give it a rest, and him too.

The sun was just breaking above the horizon as Eden, Boone, and Mason lay on their bellies near the crest of a low, sloping ridge, staring intently into the deep prairie. Their horses stood several yards behind them, chomping grass, as Old Dirty, with a wooden packsaddle strapped to his back, eyed the brothers suspiciously.

The brothers studied the small herd of buffalo grazing lazily in their direction. Waiting patiently, the three men sighted their heavy fifty-caliber Sharps rifles on the animals closest to them. They could practically taste roasted buffalo steaks, heart, and liver; a welcome change from the constant diet of beef. Besides, a cattleman doesn't like to eat his own beef—there's no profit in it.

"I say we try and get around behind 'em," said Mason, softly.

"It'll spook 'em," said Boone, just as soft.

"Let 'em get closer," added Eden. "Then we can shoot from here."

Eden took his eyes from the buffalo and stared at Boone and Mason. "I noticed you two haven't been goin' to town much lately."

Mason just shrugged and watched the buffalo.

"Got ranch things to do," answered Boone.

"Oh," said Eden, nodding. "Sure it's just ranch things?"

"What you mean?" asked Mason.

""Sure it ain't the new help?"

"Minna's gals?" said Boone.

"What are you gettin' at?" Mason asked.

"To get right to it," replied Eden, "don't you two think it's time to settle down; begin raisin' a family; have a nice home?"

"We got a nice home," said Mason.

"What do we need a family for?" added Boone.

"It'd be good for you," said Eden. "Look at me and Minna. Marriage makes a different man out of you."

"I don't want to be different," said Boone.

"Me either," said Mason.

"But opportunity is knockin'," continued Eden. "Right in your own backyard. What could be easier?"

"You talkin' about Narcissa and Leila?" asked Boone.

"Two good lookin' women," said Eden.

"True," replied Boone. "But there's lots of good lookin' women in the world."

"That's right," said Mason.

"I know," said Eden, "but they ain't here, are they?"

"I'll admit Leila is a real looker," said Mason. "But I got things to do before I get hobbled."

"Like what?" replied Eden.

"Seein' the sights," answered Mason.

"The sights of what?" asked Eden.

"Chicago for instance. That'd be like seein' another world; bein' in another world. Not to mention a lot of fancy dressed women."

"That'd be worth the trip right there," said Boone.

"Just shut up," ordered Eden. "You don't know nothin' about Chicago."

"So? Why shouldn't Mason head for Chicago if he wants to?"

"I suppose you're goin' with him?" growled Eden.

"I got different plans," replied Boone.

"Like what?"

Boone forgot about the buffalo hunt and turned on his side to face Eden. "Like turnin' this ranch into a giant. Thousands more acres; horses as far as you can see; money just rainin' down. With a life like that you can marry who you please, when you please. No sense rushin' into anything unpleasant."

"Amen to that," said Mason.

"Nobody asked for your opinion," snapped Eden.

"What exactly are you up to?" replied Mason. "Narcissa and Leila got you in the matchmakin' business?"

"Course not."

"Then why we havin' this discussion?" asked Boone. "To be honest, I'm not that taken with old Narcissa."

"And the same here about Leila," said Mason. "Why should me and Boone go off and get married?"

"Well, I did," replied Eden, starting to lose his temper more.

"That's your business," said Boone.

"My business?" shouted Eden. "Do you remember why I went and got married?"

"Settle down," said Boone, and motioned to the buffalo.

"To hell with them," yelled Eden. "I married Minna and brought her here to help us out. Now you two waddies act like it's beneath you to do the same thing."

"You're actin' like you regret it," said Boone.

"I am not," said Eden.

"Yes, you are," said Mason.

Eden stared at Mason, then Boone, then stared down questioning if maybe they weren't right. Suddenly he sprang to his feet, trying to decide what to do next.

"Get down, they'll see you," whispered Boone, pointing to the buffalo.

Eden cocked the hammer of his rifle and fired it into the air. The echo of the shot rolled across the prairie like thunder. The herd of buffalo turned as one and raced away, bawling and snorting.

"Now look what you done," yelled Mason.

Eden paid no attention, mounted his horse, and rode away.

"I think he's the one that needs a trip to Chicago," said Mason.

Boone nodded in agreement. "He's got a lot of nerve tryin' to talk us into gettin' married."

Minna had sent Narcissa and Leila to the large bunkhouse of the ranch to dust, sweep, and scrub the floors, and wash windows; not that it was something that had to be done right away, she just wanted to get them out of her hair for a while. Their minds were only focused on trapping Boone and Mason as soon as possible, and their work habits had been going rapidly downhill, and Minna found herself doing most of the chores again.

Even now, Narcissa and Leila were lying down on the job—literally. Leila was reclining on one of the bunks, thumbing through a two year old Sears and Roebuck mail order catalog she had found flung in a cobweb-covered corner. Narcissa sat comfortably in a chair with her feet up on a table, smoking a cigarette and day dreaming.

Hearing a noise outside, the two women jumped to their feet. Narcissa started waving a feather duster around while Leila pretended to sweep the floor. Narcissa worked her way to one of the windows, looked out, and saw Eden dismounting his horse near the kitchen door of the main house.

"It's just Eden," said Narcissa.

"Mason with him?" asked Leila, joining her at the window.

"Don't see him or Boone," answered Narcissa.

"What's he doing?" asked Leila.

They watched Eden pace back and forth beside his horse, then turn abruptly and walk towards the kitchen door.

Minna was taking two loaves of bread out of the oven when the kitchen door burst open and Eden entered, red-faced and agitated.

"Eden," said Minna, surprised, "I thought you and the boys were goin' to be huntin' all mornin'."

"Well, I…" Eden stopped, turned and closed the door, then walked to the kitchen table. "I been doin' some thinkin' on my way back here. Sit down, please."

"What is it?" asked Minna, and seated herself at the table.

Eden sat beside her, not sure of how to begin. "Thing is…well, I had a talk with Boone and Mason. And to get right to the point, some things were said and…and all of a sudden it hit me like a bucket of bricks."

"What did?"

"You and me. I'm beginin' to like being married to you. An awful lot. I never imagined I'd meet anybody like you; or need anybody like you. Thought I could do things all on my own and never look back. Well, I was wrong. All of a sudden I…I want to spend the rest of my life with you. All of a sudden there's a feelin' inside me I never had before. Because of you. And I hope, someday, you'll be able to feel the same about me."

"Why, Eden," said Minna, softly. She put out her hand and gently stroked his face.

They stared at each other; not wanting to speak; not knowing what to speak. There was no need to. All they wanted to do was feel something special, for the first time; need someone for the first time; truly love someone for the first time.

Awkwardly, Eden kissed Minna's hand, stood up, nodded, and walked towards the kitchen door, putting his hat back on. "Got to get back to work." He stopped and turned back. "As far as Boone and Mason are concerned you'd better tell Narcissa and Leila not to hang by their thumbs waitin' for them two muttonheads to make a move."

Eden went out, mounted his horse, and rode away. Minna stood in the doorway staring after him, her mouth half open. Suddenly became her old self again.

"Damn," she said quietly. "I really do have a husband."

Seconds later, Narcissa and Leila came hurrying into view, anxious and excited.

"Well," said Narcissa, "did he talk to Boone?"

"How about Mason?" added Leila.

Minna hesitated then walked back into the kitchen. "Don't go buyin' no weddin' dress just yet."

"Hell," said Leila, slamming the kitchen door shut.

"What do we have to do to create some interest?" said Narcissa, dropping into a chair.

"I'm not sure," replied Minna, "but we got to think of something quick. I got a husband to take care of."

"Well, what about us?" said Leila, half pouting, and took a seat at the far end of the kitchen table.

"I'm in just as big a hurry as you are," said Minna. "I'm workin' harder now than before you two showed up."

"You should have thought about that before inviting us here," said Narcissa, lighting up a cigarette.

"You got that right," replied Minna, staring down, thinking.

"Well, I don't want to end up a cranky old maid," said Leila. "I want to have fun."

"You mean you haven't been, so far?" said Narcissa, sarcastically, and blew a stream of smoke into the air.

"Well, you're goin' to," said Minna. There was a devilish look in her eyes.

"I haven't seen that expression for a long time," said Narcissa. "What are you up to?"

"Not me; you two," replied Miinna.

"Will it be fun?" asked Leila.

"It depends on you," said Minna.

The three women began to lay their plan calmly and carefully, not omitting a single detail.

CHAPTER TWELVE

The following morning, when Eden and Boone rode away to finish checking and mending the remaining miles of fence line, Mason was left at the ranch to split firewood. Though the pile was growing larger and large, there were still a lot more logs to be sawed and split before the snows came. With each new day the frost was thicker on the rooftops, more chilling winds blew in despite the glaring white sun in a cloudless sky.

Mason worked steadily, his hat and coat tossed carelessly on the ground. His sleeves were rolled up, his face, arms, and hands wet with sweat. Behind him, at one of the kitchen windows appeared Leila's face, then Narcissa's, then Minna's. They studied Mason with intense, cunning eyes. After exchanging a few words they turned away.

Leila, dressed in a worn flannel bathrobe and nightgown, and barefooted, crossed to the kitchen stove and checked the steaming kettles of water.

"Are you sure this is going to work?" she asked. "I'm beginning to feel like a ninny."

"It can't fail," said Narcissa. "You're a woman, aren't you?"

"Yeah," replied Leila, slowly, still not confident as to her part in this scheme.

"Just do like we said, and you can't fail," said Minna, taking a pan of biscuits out of the oven.

"Are we ready?" asked Narcissa, putting on her hat and coat.

"Coffee and biscuits on the table," answered Minna, then looked to Leila.

"Let me finish filling the tub," said Leila, taking one of the steaming kettles of water from the stove and pouring it into the already steaming copper bathtub beside the stove.

"Hurry it up," said Narcissa, going out the door.

"I'm hurrying, Queen of Sheba," snapped Leila.

Minna went to one of the kitchen windows and looked out.

Mason gathered up a large armload of spit wood and started for the woodshed when Narcissa made her appearance, walking casually towards the barn.

"Oh, Mason, there you are," she said, smiling.

"Need more wood for the house?" asked Mason.

"No, we're fine. Minna wanted me to tell you there's fresh coffee and biscuits on the table. Better hurry while it's hot."

"Thank you," said Mason, dropping the wood.

Narcissa continued to the barn as Mason went straight as an arrow for the house.

Soon as Mason opened the kitchen door his eyes lit up at the site of the steaming pot of coffee and fat fresh biscuits in the center of the table; his eyes then lit up a bit more when he glanced to his right and saw Leila. She was just stepping out of the copper bathtub with only a small, thin towel covering her—just enough to keep from being arrested. The water running down her perfectly formed legs, arms, and shoulders added immensely to her allure. She acted surprised, then embarrassed, but kept her perfect pose.

Mason stood there like a stump; mouth open, eyes glazed over—hypnotized almost. Finally the shock wore off and all he could think of doing was grabbing his hat off his head, mumbling an apology, and turning quickly to leave—too quickly. He slammed, full-face, into the edge of the open door, fell backwards to the floor, and never moved.

Now it was Leila's turn to stand there shocked and open-mouthed.

"Minna!" she yelled in a panic. "Minna, get in here!"

Minna came running out of her bedroom and down the hallway to the kitchen. She found Leila standing by the tub still wrapped in the thin towel and pointing. It was then Minna noticed Mason on the floor.

"What the hell'd you do?" shouted Minna.

"Nothing. The dumb ox walked into the door."

"This is all I need," grumbled Minna, crossing to Mason and looking down at him.

"He ain't dead, it he?" asked Leila, hurrying over.

"Get some clothes on you naked savage," ordered Minna.

It took a bit of doing for Minna, Leila, and Narcissa to drag Mason out of the kitchen, down the hallway to his room, and hoist him onto his bed. When they rolled him on his back his spurs snagged one of the blankets and wrapped around him like a newborn babe in swaddling clothes.

"Well, this changes everything," said Narcissa in disgust.

"No, it don't," said Minna, thinking hard on how to correct the situation.

"This whole thing is ruined now," said Leila, throwing her hands up.

"This is better than we planned," replied Minna. "Get that robe off."

"Why?" asked Leila, clutching her robe to herself.

"Get it off!"

Once the robe was discarded, Leila's curved, lean body showed itself to spectacular advantage beneath the thin flannel nightgown. Minna adjusted the shoulders a little, and looked Leila up and down.

"You're perfect," said Minna.

"Really?" said Leila, her face brightening, and her posture straightening.

"What about the sleeping Prince?" Narcissa asked.

"He's not much good unconscious," replied Minna.

"Wait," said Narcissa, walked to the nearby dresser, picked up a small wash cloth, and dipped it into a pitcher of water setting in a porcelain basin. After wringing it out, she flung it across the room hitting Mason full in the face.

The women waited, and finally Mason began to revive with a low moan.

"The rest is up to you," said Minna to Leila.

She and Narcissa hurried out, closing the bedroom door.

When Mason pulled the wet cloth from his face his vision was slightly blurred, and his head throbbed. He thought he saw an angel at the foot of the bed dressed in diaphanous white, with reddish golden hair flowing about her shoulders, sparkling green eyes, and the robust figure of a goddess. Then Leila broke the spell.

"You alive?" she asked loudly.

"What…happened? How'd I get here?"

"Wasn't easy," replied Leila. "Thought we might have to drag you in here with the mule."

Leila sat on the edge of the bed gently. "Mind if I sit here, the floor's kind of cold?" She pulled her knees up close to her firm breast, which were tempting dark shadows beneath the white flannel.

Mason swallowed hard and kept staring. Leila rubbed her feet to warm them. Mason stared some more. Leila noticed. She pulled the hem of her nightgown up above her smooth knees. Her silky legs were perfect. She flapped the hem of her nightgown roughly.

"I feel flushed," she said. "Guess it was the hot bath."

"You sure smell good," said Mason, softly.

"That's the rose water I put in. I just love that scent. Don't you?"

Mason could only nod.

Leila leaned forward on one arm, and the front of her nightgown fell dangerously low. Mason tried to sit up straight and not look, but he was still trapped in the tangle of blanket.

"You sure you're all right, Mason?"

"Yes, ma'am. Thank you."

Leila played with her long hair, saying, "I'll bet my hair looks like it was beat with a broom; it's from all that steamy water."

"No. You look…beautiful."

"Stop. That's not true."

Mason could only stare.

"I said, that's not true," repeated Leila, wanting an encouraging answer.

"Yes, it is," replied Mason, nodding rapidly. "You're absolutely…"

"You're going to make me blush," said Leila, starting to move across the foot of the bed on her hands and knees, her nightgown pulled firmly around her small buttocks. When she got to the far side of the bed she stopped and smiled at Mason.

"You sure you're all right?" she asked.

Mason opened his mouth, but no words came out.

"I better get to my room and get some clothes on. People might start to talk."

Mason nodded weakly. He watched Leila move gracefully to the doorway, stop, and turn. She stared at him, letting him get a final last look then waved her fingers shyly and went out.

Mason looked lost, helpless, and defenseless. His face was beet-red, his pulse rapid, and sweat was beading on his forehead. He took the wet cloth, he still clutched, and mopped his face.

The next day it was Boone's turn to make a fool out of himself at the foot of the Throne of Woman.

Eden and Mason had gone to town for supplies, leaving Boone to continue sawing logs and splitting them into stove wood. As planned, the kitchen window swung open and Minna's smiling face appeared. Leila came up behind her, wanting to see what was going on, but Minna shoved her away.

"Boone," called Minna, sweetly. "Could you go to the barn and see what's keepin' Narcissa? I need her here."

"Be glad to," replied Boone, throwing his axe down.

Like Mason, the day before, his coat was off, his sleeves rolled up, his face and arms sweaty. Walking towards the barn, he flexed his broad shoulders and held his arms out to let the wind blow across him to cool him. He breathed deeply and smiled, unaware of what awaited him beyond the wide open doors of the barn.

Narcisssa was in the hayloft, leaning on a long-handled pitch fork, daydreaming, when she heard the sound of spurs approaching. She went quickly to the half-open door of the hayloft and began forking out clumps of hay to a band of anxious horses waiting below in the small corral. Old Dirty, the mule, was too stubborn to leave the comfort of the barn, and stood looking up at the hayloft, making strange moaning noises, trying to attract Narcissa's attention, and get his share of feed. But Narcissa still hadn't changed her opinion of him, and ignored him.

Boone climbed almost to the top of the hayloft ladder and stuck his head up through the open flooring. Narcissa pretended not to notice. She was without a hat and coat, and her dark red work dress clung to her in thin delicate folds outlining her lean, but muscular form. Her sleeves were rolled up, and the front of her dress was unbuttoned past her large breasts that bulged against a tight black bodice of intricate lace.

Boone started to say something but stopped. The shaft of sunlight slanting in over the top of the hayloft door seemed to form a luminous glow around Narcissa. Her black hair had a fascinating bluish cast as it caressed her face and flowed around the base of her smooth white neck. She was magnificent in the light. A hard-working cowboy rarely saw anything like that inside a barn, and he didn't want to spoil it.

Narcissa got impatient waiting for Boone to move, or say something, and she turned with a look of surprise.

"Why, Boone," she said breathless, "I didn't know you were there."

"Didn't mean to startle you," replied Boone. "Minna said she needs you at the house."

"Another chore, I imagine," said Narcissa, coldly. "It must have been hell here after she moved in."

"Workin' you hard, is she?" asked Boone, concerned.

"Wouldn't surprise me she sends me out to pick cotton tomorrow."

Boone came further up the ladder. "You want me to feed the horses for you?"

"No, no. I have to earn my keep; just like the mule." Narcissa forced a smile.

Boone smiled back, saying, "Sure is a pretty dress."

"It's just a rag," replied Narcissa, standing erect and swaying her hips from side to side, her breasts bulging. "It's from my time working on the stage."

Boone was puzzled for a second. "You drove a stagecoach?"

Narcissa's eyebrows went up, Boone's innocent remark cutting deep.

"No. I was in the theater. An actress."

Boone's mouth fell open and he came up into the loft, fascinated by what Narcissa had just revealed.

"Well, I…Minna never said nothin' about that. What was it like?"

"Oh, you'll just be bored," said Narcissa, swinging her hips carelessly now, her Thespian pride flooding out of her. "It's a long story. But fascinating. I'll have to perform for you some evening."

"Perform?"

"A scene from one of the plays I was in. I even wrote one. It's brilliant."

"You're amazing," said Boone, completely taken with her now.

Narcissa moved to Boone in a smooth, long-legged stride and stopped, their bodies almost touching. Boone could smell her lilac perfume for the first time, and he felt a weakness rush over him. Narcissa gently brushed some tiny wood chips out of the whisker stubble on his cheek. He couldn't take his eyes from hers, not until he noticed her breasts moving in and out in a subtle rhythm. He suddenly started backing away towards the hayloft ladder.

"I better…get to…" he began awkwardly. "I'll tell Minna…"

"Yes, tell her I'll be right there, if I don't have a stroke first," said Narcissa, moving towards the hayloft door.

Boone started to turn to the ladder when Narcissa let out a quick cry. He spun around to her. "What's wrong?"

Narcissa angrily threw the pitchfork down. "I think I stuck myself."

She pulled one side of her dress clear up to her hip, revealing the most beautiful leg Boone had ever seen—not even on the best horse he'd ever owned.

"Am I bleeding? Narcissa asked, looking as if she were going to cry.

"I don't see anything," said Boone, swallowing hard.

"Are you sure?" Narcissa hiked her dress higher, and shoved the hayloft door all the way open for more light.

The sunlight streamed down on her like the shaft of a huge spotlight, and the long, mesmerizing leg seemed to be made of satin instead of skin.

"Take a closer look."

Boone could only back away, again, unsure of what to say or do. A gentleman doesn't look at a ladies leg no matter how perfect it is. But he should have been more concerned of where he was going. The hayloft floor ended abruptly and Boone dropped out of sight. Luckily, his fall was broken when he landed across the rump of Old Dirty, standing directly below him. The snorting sorehead was expecting hay to come down, not something with arms and legs. Old Dirty's instinct for survival blossomed, and Boone was catapulted through the air and into the far wall.

Narcissa hurried to the edge of the loft and stared down. "Jesus, Mary, Joseph," she gasped.

Climbing down, Narcisssa rushed to Boone who was trying to get to his feet, but couldn't. His eyes looked a little crossed, and his hat was jammed firmly over his ears. Narcissa put her arm around him and let him lean against her. Old Dirty stood close watching with great interest, almost like he wanted to help, then snorted and walked away.

"Boone, honey, you all right?" asked Narcissa, pulling his hat up off his ears so he wouldn't look like he was wearing a bucket. He stared at her and smiled drunkenly.

"You smell sweeter than the prairie in summer time," he mumbled.

"Why thank you. I didn't think you noticed."

"I couldn't help but notice."

Narcissa's face lit up and she began running her fingers through Boone's thick, curly hair.

"Your hair's so silky," she said, seductively.

Boone laid his cheek against her plump breast and closed his eyes. Narcissa waited a respectable time.

"Well, I think that's enough for today." Narcissa began pulling Boone to his feet. "You better get back to what you were doing."

Boone blinked his eyes and revived somewhat more. "Yeah. Better do those chores." He was a little wobbly, and kept staring at Narcissa.

"You behave now," said Narcissa, and started Boone towards the open doors of the barn, giving him a slap on the rump.

CHAPTER THIRTEEN

After their encounters with Leila and Narcissa, Mason and Boone began to change. Eden, Chunk Bascom, and Billy Birdsong were the first to notice. It was one evening at the line shack when Eden and his brothers had ridden over for a friendly game of poker. They were all gathered around the only table in the place, and sitting on short stools or frail, warped chairs.

The wind off the prairie was howling against the thickly chinked log walls, but the big iron stove was glowing red, its load of wood snapping and popping every so often, keeping the cold at bay. A large kerosene lamp hung low from a rater of the sod roof directly over the scarred table. Chunk was shuffling the cards, which looked tiny in his thick, gnarly hands.

"You won that one, Eden," said Chunk. "But I'm feelin' lucky this hand."

Billy poured some whiskey into a cup from a bottle on the table, downed it with a jerk of his head, and made a grim face.

"Sure glad you brought this, Eden," gasped Billy. "Goin' to be a frosty one tonight."

"Just save some for the rest of us," said Chunk, dealing the cards.

"What are the women folk up to?" asked Billy, pouring another drink.

"Whatever they want," replied Eden, picking up his cards. "Thought we'd get out of their hair a while. Let 'em get to know each other better, without us around."

Chunk studied his cards, saying, "Billy, here, said them two new hires were real lookers."

"I'd give four horses for both of them any day," said Billy.

Chunk glanced at Boone and Mason, who simply sat their with their cards in their hands, not really looking at them.

"You two playin' or starin'?" asked Chunk.

Boone and Mason glanced up, saw everyone was watching. They each tossed a coin into the center of the table. The others did the same.

"They don't look so good," Billy whispered to Eden.

Eden shrugged. "Been like that all day. Like talkin' to a tree stump half the time."

"It's the change in the weather," said Chunk. "Wind come across the prairie and knifes straight through your heart."

"I think it's more their heads," said Eden.

"Medicine man can fix 'em," said Billy. "Take 'em to the reservation."

"Two for me," said Chunk, dealing himself the cards.

"Three," said Billy.

"One," said Eden.

Chunk dealt the new cards then waited for Boone and Mason to say something. They just stared at their cards like before. Billy tapped a finger to his head as he looked at Chunk. Chunk nodded in agreement.

"Every so often this big old prairie, and that big old sky, gets to a man," said Chunk, softly. "Does funny things to you."

"Well, somethin's got to them," said Eden, studying his cards. "That's for sure."

Boone and Mason never heard a word.

In the brightly lighted kitchen of the ranch house, Minna and Narcissa were finishing scrubbing and drying the pots, pans, and dishes from supper, while Leila sang softly and swept the floor, happy in her thoughts.

"I still can't get over how much those three can eat," said Narcissa, wiping a large skillet.

"Haven't let up any since I been here," said Minna.

"Good thing they own a lot of cows," added Narcissa.

Leila moved past them still singing to herself and still sweeping.

"What are you so dreamy about?" asked Narcissa.

Leila turned. "Just thinking about Mason. I like him a lot. He reminds me of one of those dashing heroes in the Three Musketeers story." She went back to sweeping and smiling.

"What about Boone?" said Minna to Narcissa. "He remind you of a Musketeer?"

"More like some rascal out of a Charles Dickens book," replied Narcissa. "But a nice rascal. Handsome to boot. Even when he was lying against the wall in the barn, helpless."

"Yes," said Leila, "that's the way Mason looked after he walked into the door."

"Well, try and keep them on their feet from now on," said Minna. "Or you're never goin' to get anywhere with 'em."

"What's this?" asked Leila.

Minna and Narcissa watched as Leila reached behind a large flour barrel, in the far corner, and pulled out a two gallon jug with a fat cork in the top. Leila set the jug on the kitchen table and the women gathered around it. Narcissa struggle to get the cork out, then sniffed at the contents. Her eyes lit up.

"Get some cups," she ordered.

At first, the women only put a small amount of whiskey into their cups—just a sample—to make sure it wasn't spoiled.

"Wonder where they got this stuff?" said Minna.

"Got a zip to it," said Narcissa.

"Should we be doin' this?" asked Leila.

"Just havin' a taste, is all," replied Minna.

"Besides we earned it," said Narcissa. "Working like root hogs all day."

The three sat at the table with the fat jug in front of them, and began to relax.

"I sure like it out here, Minna," began Leila, cheerfully. "I'm sure glad you sent that telegram to meet Narcissa in Saint Joe. I was beginning to think I was destined to spend my life an old maid schoolmarm."

"Weren't there any men around?" Narcissa asked, smacking her lips.

"Just dumb ones, and married ones. And the married ones weren't inhibited about making eyes at each others wives. And their kids acted like they had their upbringing from the devil himself. One day, in class, one of them bit me on the leg just cause he felt like it."

"You give him what he deserved?" asked Narcissa.

"I'll say. That's why I got fired. Thank God."

The women drank a little more; put a little more in their cups, and began to feel a little more relaxed.

"Well, if you think you had it bad," said Narcissa, after a long swallow, "you should have been with me, in the wonderful world of the theater."

"But you always loved play actin'," said Minna, taking a quick sip.

"But I didn't count on play acting on sleazy riverboats, and saloons full of drunken, leering baboons. That manager of ours had a knack for booking us into the worst hell-holes on both sides of the Missouri river. Luckily, he got killed in a poker game, or who knows where we would have all ended up." She patted Minna gently on the hand. "When your telegram caught up with me I lit out faster than a frightened humming bird."

Narcissa drained her cup and so did Minna and Leila. Narcissa stood up, put the heavy jug under her arm, and began refilling the cups—only fuller this time.

"Won't hurt to have a touch more," said Narcissa.

"What about you, Minna?" said Leila. "Last we saw you, you said it was California or bust. Now here you are."

Minna took a quick gulp. "Yeah, I know. Had big dreams of reaching California and striking gold like everybody else, or striking a rich husband. But things got changed around a bit. Like I didn't have any control over it. There I was, earnin' my keep, one day, and when I looked up there was this handsome cowboy standin' there."

"Eden?" said Leila, smiling.

"Eden. Sounds silly, but once we got to talkin' I got a feelin' he was the one. Don't ask me why. But that's just the way it happened. Just standin' there talkin'. Maybe you can explain it to me. And there I went, ridin' out of town a married woman. I'm still tryin' to figure it all out."

"Here's to love," said Narcissa, raising her cup.

The three clinked cups and drank.

"I hope Mason'll come to love me," said Leila, filling her own cup now. "What about you and Boone, Narcissa?"

"Oh, I'm not planning on running away from him," replied Narcissa, holding out her cup. "But I need some time to think things over better."

"Well, don't think too long," said Minna, holding out her cup, which Leila filled. "You don't want his interest to fade. Him and Mason go into town a lot. You could end up havin' some stiff competition."

"Oh, I think Leila and I are up to the challenge," said Narcissa. "Right, Lei?"

"And then some," answered Leila in a determined voice. "I'm not letting Mason get loose no how. You should have seen him when I left him in his room that day. He was sweating good."

"And when Boone staggered out of the barn," said Narcissa, "He had a confused, glazed look in his eyes. That was encouraging."

"You can't rest on your laurels," said Minna. "I'm not sayin' don't let them make the next move, but you have to give them a little help. You two keep doin' your share and I'll keep addin' mine."

"Such as?" asked Narcissa.

"Never mind. Just be ready to go along with whatever I do. You don't want them to bolt when you almost got 'em in the corral."

"Well, I'm ready," said Leila, a little unsteady in her chair.

"To get married?" asked Narcissa.

"No. For another touch of whiskey."

Minna and Narcissa nodded, and held out their cups for a refill.

CHAPTER FOURTEEN

It was a subdued breakfast the next morning—the women slow and touchy from the aftermath of overflowing cups of whiskey that would have made a rabbit attack a coyote. Eden and his brothers couldn't help noticing the change in the women, but they weren't sure what to make of it.

Some of the grub wasn't exactly up to par, and the coffee was barely warm, and a touch weak. However, the brothers had learned early on not to complain to the cook unless you wanted to go hungry, or be subject to a lot of unkind words. Besides that, Boone and Mason didn't have food on their minds—far from it. Their faces were shaved smooth as glass, hair combed and slicked down; and they were wearing new shirts, pants, and bandannas. Their boots even had a polish, and their spurs shined. But Narcissa and Leila never noticed. Boone and Mason began to feel anxious, and were fast losing their appetite; the spark seemed to have gone out of the budding relationships. The boys hardly touched their grub.

After breakfast everyone went their separate, quiet ways; Eden to the parlor to work on the ranch account books, Boone and Mason to the corral to saddle their horses, but their hearts weren't in it.

Minna, Narcissa, and Leila stood at the kitchen stove drinking thick, black coffee, waiting for a big kettle to boil to do the day's laundry.

"This coffee isn't improving the taste in my mouth any," mumbled Narcissa. "I think I better sit down."

"No," said Minna, sternly, then looked towards the parlor to see if Eden was still there, and spoke softly. "Go on out and do your chores just like we planned. Leila you stay here and help me get the laundry started."

"I need to go rest," muttered Leila, her eyes half closed.

"You just stay where you are," said Minna, and shoved her against the wall. "Narcissa, get goin'."

Narcissa dropped her empty cup on top the stove and shuffled to her hat and coat hanging on a peg beside the kitchen door. She struggled into them then stood there.

"I don't feel in a romantic mood just yet," she said half-heartedly.

"Well, get romantic," ordered Minna.

Narcissa went out slamming the door.

As Boone and Mason finished saddling their horses, in the main corral, Boone caught sight of Narcissa emerging from the barn with a wooden bucket in her hand. She still had a shuffling walk, and no interest whatsoever in feeding the flock of chickens that followed her. She haphazardly tossed handfuls of cracked corn from the bucket, and wandered aimlessly. It didn't take long for Boone to hurry over, hat in hand, and all smiles.

"Here, let me do that," he said, grabbing the heavy bucket.

"Thank you," said Narcissa, and threw a handful of corn at the chickens as if trying to drive them away. "You people always work this hard, this early?"

"Yep. No gettin' around it. Seven days a week. You ain't seen nothin' yet. Wait till spring roundup."

"God Almighty," mumbled Narcissa, and shuffled to the well.

"Yep," said Boone, leaning against the well so he could get a good look at Narcissa, while the chickens stared at him just as hard. "Ma and Pa worked from sunup to sundown. Rain or shine, windstorm or blizzard. Had a full life, but died young."

"Doesn't surprise me," replied Narcissa, raising the water bucket to her lips. She took a big gulp and groaned with relief.

"You sure look nice this mornin'," said Boone, softly.

Narcissa lowered the bucket and gasped, "Thank you", and continued drinking.

"But if you don't mind my sayin', you look a touch haggard."

"I feel a touch haggard," said Narcissa between gulps.

"If Minna's workin' you too hard I could have a word with her."

"That'd be like talking to a fence post," said Narcissa, and set the bucket down. She looked at Boone then smiled. "But that's awful sweet of you, Boone."

"I'd be more than happy to do it."

"You're quite the charming man. I'm glad we met. I really am."

Boone stood up tall and threw his shoulders back. "And I feel the same about you. I was thinkin' maybe…"

"Narcissa!"

Minna's harsh tone shattered the gentle moment.

Narcissa turned her head submissively. "What?"

Minna stood at the side of the ranch house, sleeves rolled up and her blouse spotted dark from water and soap suds. "I need your help, right now."

Narcissa started away then turned to Boone. "Maybe we can talk later. Hopefully."

"Hurry up," yelled Minna.

"I'm coming," Narcissa yelled as she walked on.

A frown came to Boone's face as he watched Narcissa shuffle towards an impatient Minna. "Minna sure is gettin' uppity," he muttered.

Minutes later, Mason got his chance to be alone with Leila. She was out back of the ranch house hanging laundry, which wasn't easy as the wind had picked up and was snapping, shirts, pants, long johns, and dresses every which way.

Mason trotted up beside her on his horse, dismounted, and took the heavy laundry basket from her with a smile.

"Let me hold that for you."

"Why thank you," smiled Leila, then frowned and closed her eyes as a stabbing pain filled her forehead.

"You sick?" asked Mason, deeply concerned.

"No, no. Just didn't get much sleep. I'll be fine."

"Why don't you sit down and rest a minute."

"I got to get this stuff hung. Minna's got more coming."

"All you seem to do lately is laundry."

"I know. It's like working in a Chinese laundry around here. I'm going to be worn down to a stub."

"Well, I was thinkin' about that."

"Really?" said Leila, continuing to hang clothes.

"You should ask Minna for some time off. Go into town and see the sites. I sure know some good ones."

"Oh, I'd love too, but Minna needs me here."

"Every single hour?"

"It seems that way, don't it?"

"Don't you ever get lonely, want to do somethin' different?

"Sometimes," said Leila, sadly. "Then I think maybe I'll just get a dog."

"Dogs don't do too good out here," said Mason, shaking his head.

"No?"

"We had three, a while back. The wolves got 'em."

"All three?"

Mason nodded.

"Maybe I'll get a cat then."

"Hawks'll get 'em."

"What kind of place is this?"

"I think the best thing is for you to see the sites in town."

"Exactly what kind of sights?" said Leila, starting to flirt, even though the whiskey haze hadn't abated much. But she was able to force a painful smile.

Mason stared, not sure if she was about to have some sort of fit.

"You know," continued Leila, "I'm not like those painted women you see hanging around objectionable places, Mr. McKenna."

"Oh, no, ma'am," replied Mason quickly. "Didn't mean that at all."

Leila shook her finger at him. "I'm starting to get the impression you might be flirting with me."

Mason gave a shy smile. "Would…would you be offended it I did?"

"Well, I…"

"Leila!"

Leila and Mason turned quicky. Minna stood at the far corner of the house, sleeves still rolled up, and more water spots and soap suds on her dress. Her hair was clinging to her sweaty face.

"How long's it take you to do that?" Minna continued in a sour tone.

"I'll be right there," replied Leila, stamping her foot. She emptied her pockets of all clothes pins and tossed them into the laundry basket. "I better go," she continued. "Can you finish this for me?"

"Finish?" said Mason, then stood there with the laundry basket, watching Leila follow Minna around towards the front of the house. He looked down at the basket, then the clothes snapping in the wind on the rope clothes line. He slowly, and awkwardly, began hanging the laundry.

Boone came riding up and reined his horse to a quick stop. Mason threw down a handful of clothes pins and stepped away from the basket.

"What the hell are you doin'?" asked Boone.

"I was…just helpin'."

"I never thought I'd live to see a cowboy doin' a load of laundry."

"Leila needed help," said Mason, defensively. "Minna's workin' her like a slave."

Boone glanced towards the house, thought a moment, and said, "She's doin' the same to Narcissa."

"It ain't right," said Mason.

"No. Minna acts like she owns them. I hardly said two words to Narcissa when Minna comes chargin' in snortin' and pawin' the ground."

"Did the same to me and Leila."

"I'm thinkin' we ought to have a talk with Eden," said Boone. "See if he can rein her in a might."

"That's a good idea," replied Mason, nodding. "But we better go easy. Old Eden's startin' to worship the ground Minna treads on."

"Sad, ain't it," said Boone, "when a man starts actin' like that?"

Eden, hat on and coat buttoned, was almost out the kitchen door when Minna hurried up behind him, taking him by the arm and walking him out.

"I need to talk to you," she said softly.

"Sure thing."

Minna motioned for him to wait, and as she started to close the kitchen door, glanced at Narcissa and Leila, who stood beside the hot stove with tub and washboard, starting to scrub a pile of dirty socks.

"Scrub everything good," she said.

As the door closed, Narcissa and Leila mumbled a sullen reply.

"Somethin' troublin' you, Minna?"

"Well, I don't want to start any unpleasantness, but it's Boone and Mason."

"What'd they do?"

Minna frowned and forced herself to go on—according to plan. "Well...they're...startin' to take up a lot of Narcissa's and Leila's time."

"They are?"

"Afraid so. And the girls are startin' to get a little distracted in their chores."

"I didn't know."

"Maybe you could talk to the boys. Ask them not to take up so much of the girls' time. I wouldn't want to have to let them go for not doin' their work. Then I'd be right back where I was."

"No, we can't have that," said Eden, concerned. "Not with the baby comin'."

"Exactly. So maybe they could give the girls a little more elbow room; not take up so much of their time."

"Don't you worry, I'll take care of it right now."

"Thank you, Eden." Minna gave him a quick kiss on the cheek. "See you at supper."

As Eden came around the far corner of the house, Boone and Mason came riding towards him leading Eden's horse.

"Got you saddled up and ready to go," said Boone.

"Then let's get at it," said Eden, mounting his horse.

"Feel's like snow in the air," said Mason, looking at the sky.

"That's why I want that south herd moved in closer. A bad storm could scatter them more than they are."

"Well, it's a long ride," began Boone, "let's..."

"Just one thing," interrupted Eden. "Seems you two got more on your mind than just ranchin'."

Boone and Mason glanced at each other then back to Eden.

"Such as?" said Boone.

"Women," replied Eden.

"What do you mean?" asked Mason, puzzled.

"You know what I mean," said Eden.

"What are you gettin' at?" Boone asked.

"You're interferin' with Minna's help."

"There's interferin', all right," said Boone, "but it ain't from us."

"Minna wants you both to back off a bit," said Eden. "Let the girls get their work done."

"So what are we supposed to do?" Mason asked. "Quit talkin' to them?"

"For a while, yeah," answered Eden.

Mason sat there with his mouth open. Boone leaned forward in his saddle, running his eyes up one side of Eden and down the other.

"What are you lookin' at?"

"I was just tryin' to see where Minna put her brand on you."

"What the hell's that mean?" said Eden, loudly.

"Just what you think it does," replied Boone, starting to lose his temper.

"Boone's right," snapped Mason. "Minna's puttin' the spurs to you good, ain't she?"

"Look, now," said Eden in a warning tone, "I don't want to get in an argument over this, so let's..."

"If I want to talk to Narcissa," interrupted Boone, "I'll talk to her."

"Me too," said Mason, getting angry. "I mean I'll talk to Leila, not..."

"And I say you won't," ordered Eden.

"And who made you the Emperor of China?" replied Boone, and rode away.

"Yeah," added Mason, following Boone.

"Get back here," yelled Eden. "We ain't done!"

Boone and Mason rode on without looking back. Eden put spurts to his horse and raced after them.

The kitchen door opened and Minna, Narcissa, and Leila stepped out onto the porch, drying their hands and arms with clean white flour sacks. They stood watching the three brothers charge off across the prairie, Eden's shouts fading in the wind.

"You sure we should be going about things this way?" asked Leila.

"Well, you just heard what Boone and Mason said," answered Minna. "They're not about to stay away or ignore you girls."

"I think this is going just right," said Narcissa, taking a cigarette and matches from her apron pocket. "As a matter of face we need to put some frosting on this cake."

"I agree," said Minna. "And I know just how to do it."

"Poor Mason. He sounded so upset," said Leila, staring off into the prairie in hopes of getting one last glimpse of him.

"So what more do we do?" said Narcissa, blowing a long stream of cigarette smoke.

"This evenin'," began Minna, "after you help me get supper started, go to your room and start packin'."

"Where we going?" asked Leila, not liking the idea.

"Nowhere?" replied Minna.

With smoke drifting lazily out of every chimney in the ranch house, Eden, Boone, and Mason returned from their day's work. No words passed between them as they curried and fed their horses, then made their separate ways to the house. All three had sulked all day. Chunk Bascom and Billy Birdsong had been helping haze the large herd of cattle out of the south range, and had sensed something was wrong, but decided to mind their own business.

Once inside the warm kitchen, the brothers began to wash up in the pans of hot water Minna had ready and waiting.

"When you're done," said Minna, busy at the cook stove, "there's hot coffee and cups on the table. You must be froze."

"Warm weather's over," sighed Eden. "That's for sure."

Minna watched closely as the brothers moved to the long kitchen table, poured themselves some coffee and sat down—Eden at one end, Boone at the other, and Mason in the middle. They sipped their coffee in silence.

Minna shook her head at their stubbornness towards each other. She felt sort of bad she had cause the situation, but it was something that had to be done. She had to keep Boone and Mason moving closer, and quicker, into the waiting arms of Narcissa and Leila. And at the same time let the two brothers think it was their idea. Their rebellion at Eden's interference was a leap forward to the conclusion of her plan. She began humming to herself, rattling pots and pans on the stove, to bring attention to herself. Finally Eden spoke.

"Where's all your help got to?"

"Oh, they're in their room. Packin'."

Boone and Mason sat up straight, staring at Minna. They wanted to ask "why?", but refused to let Eden see they were concerned or even interested.

"Packin' for what?" Eden asked.

Minna busied herself at the stove for a few seconds then turned. The three brothers sat staring at her. Their interest was more than obvious. Her audience now hung on every word.

"Well, I got to thinkin'," began Minna, walking to the table and sitting down. "I don't feel it's proper for the girls to be stayin' here in the house."

"Why not?" said Boone, his forehead wrinkled from a frown.

"It's just not proper," replied Minna.

"Why not?" Mason asked, his forehead just as wrinkled.

"Ladies don't live like this," said Minna.

"Like what?" said Boone.

"Way out here and single. In a house full of men. I should have put them in the bunkhouse the first day they came."

"Bunkhouse?" said Mason, loudly. "That drafty old barn's no place to..."

"It'll be fine," interrupted Minna. "And it'll only be till spring round up. Then they'll be gone."

"Gone?" said Boone, a little too loud. "What for?"

"I'm sure they don't want to stay here forever," said Minna. "Afterall, they're attractive young women, they must have all kinds of plans."

"What kind of plans?" asked Mason, his face red with anxiety.

"I don't know," answered Minna, shrugging. "They haven't talked much, and I don't pry, but I'm sure they have thoughts of settlin' down somewhere nice, gettin' married, havin' a fine home just like this one."

"You think so?" said Boone, his mind racing.

"It wouldn't surprise me," continued Minna, "next time they go to town, some smooth talkin' fellas will sweep them off their feet, and that'll be the last we see of them."

Boone and Mason stared at one another, worry and fear sweeping over them.

"Then your help would be gone," said Eden.

"I know," said Minna, "But we can get other help. A hired man this time. Maybe I should do that anyway. Let the girls go and hire a man."

Boone and Mason stared at Minna now, looking as if they wanted to string her up from the nearest tree.

"What do you think I should do, Eden?" she asked.

"Whatever you feel is right. We can always pay them off, and take 'em to town. Just say the word."

Boone and Mason turned their hard eyes to Eden, wondering if they should hang him from the same limb as Minna.

Narcissa and Leila paraded into the kitchen, hats and coats on, and carrying their bulging carpet bags.

"Evening," said Narcissa, a bright smile on her face.

"All set, Minna," said Leila, also with a bright smile.

"Fine," replied Minna, getting up and going back to the stove. "You gals go get yourselves settled."

Boone and Mason watched the two women move to the door as if they were leaving permanently.

"Supper will be ready soon," said Minna.

"We'll be here," said Narcissa, going out.

Leila gave Mason a quick wave of her hand. All he could do was nod, not wanting her to go.

After the door closed, Minna busied herself with the cooking, and began humming. Boone and Mason sat glowering at Eden. He took a couple gulps of coffee before he noticed.

"What's wrong now?" asked Eden.

Boone and Mason looked away, refusing to answer.

"Oh," said Minna, surprise in her voice. "I almost forgot. They'll need their trunks over there. Could you…"

Boone and Mason jumped up and hurried down the hallway to the far bedroom.

The bunkhouse was well lighted as Narcissa and Leila began to make themselves comfortable. Three kerosene lamps illuminated the large sleeping quarters and the tall cast iron stove. The wind rattled the windows and whistled through a few thin cracks in the rough board walls, but the hot stove threw a satisfying warmth from floor to ceiling.

The women had their hats and coats off, and their open carpet bags set on a long wooden table in the center of the room.

"I hope Minna knows what she's doing," said Narcissa, unpacking. "I sure don't want to stay in this dusty rat hole very long."

"Did you see Mason's face when we left?" said Leila, searching through her bag. "He looked like he was going to cry."

"So will I if Boone doesn't make a move soon," replied Narcissa, and lit a cigarette. "We might be playing a little too hard to get."

"You think so?" Leila asked, looking worried. "That wouldn't be good, would it?"

Just then there were thumping noises on the bunkhouse porch, then a knock on the door.

"Can we come in?" Boone called loudly.

"I spoke too soon," said Narcissa, throwing her cigarette down and stamping on it.

Leila ran to the door and opened it. Boone and Mason, each shouldering a heavy trunk, entered smiling.

"We thought you might need these," said Boone.

"Thank you so much," said Leila, smiling and closing the door against a driving wind.

"Right over there will be fine," said Narcissa, motioning to beside the table.

"Sure hope you'll be comfortable here," said Mason as he and Bone set the trunks down, and took off their hats.

"I'll bring in some extra firewood before we leave," said Boone.

"Me, too," said Mason, looking at Leila.

"I'm sure sorry you had to move into this boar's nest," said Boone.

"Well, now that you mention it," said Narcissa, "it was quite a shock when Minna told us we had to move. Wasn't it Leila?"

"What?" said Leila, her concentration still on Mason's handsome face. "Oh, yes," she said quickly, and walked over beside Narcissa. "Yes, quite a shock. Never thought Minna would do this."

"She changed all of a sudden," said Narcissa. "Right after we began working here."

"Real bossy," said Leila.

"Eden, too," said Mason.

"Just between us," began Narcissa, "Leila and I were discussing whether to stay or not. Weren't we Leila?"

"Yes. It's not right being treated this way."

"Well, don't do nothin' hasty," said Boone. "You can work somethin' out."

"I'm not so sure," answered Narcissa.

"We could talk to Minna," said Mason, anxiously, "get her to settle down a bit."

"I don't know," replied Narcissa, shrugging. "Maybe we should just go."

"No," said Boone and Mason.

Narcissa started putting some of her clothes back into her carpet bag, then Leila starting doing the same.

"How far is it to town?" Leila asked.

"Real far," said Mason, hoping to stop her from packing.

"It's too late now, anyway," added Boone. "It's gettin' darker out by the minute."

"We could probably get perfectly good jobs in town," said Narcissa, still packing.

"Better," said Leila, packing also.

"And get married to boot," Narcissa said to no one in particular.

"But you got good jobs right here," said Boone.

"But we're not married," replied Narcissa.

"And that's a fact," said Leila.

"We'll marry you," Mason blurted out.

Mason and Boone looked at each other, neither one sure if they heard right. Turning their heads slowly, they found the two women staring back calmly, a slight smile on their faces, and very sure of themselves now.

"You sure you're both sober?" Narcissa asked.

"Sober as a preacher on Sunday," answered Boone.

"Me, too," said Mason.

"This is so sudden," said Leila, coyly, trying to act embarrassed.

"But what would Minna and Eden say?" asked Narcissa.

"It's none of their business," replied Boone.

"That's right," said Mason. "It's our business."

"We're grow'd men," added Boone. "We can do what we please."

"And we're grow'd women," said Leila.

"Well, what are we waiting for," said Narcissa. "Town can't be that far away, can it?"

"Or a justice of the peace, either," said Leila.

Boone and Mason turned to each other for encouragement; waiting for the other to say something.

"Well?" Mason finally said.

"Let's do it," answered Boone, loudly.

Leila began jumping up and down and clapping her hands.

Eden was still seated at the kitchen table sipping coffee and watching Minna set out plates for supper. They both heard the loud whinny of a horse then the sound of hoofs. Eden crossed quickly to the door, followed by Minna. Stepping to the edge of the porch they watched Boone and Mason ride quickly up to the bunkhouse. Narcissa and Leila came running out, their coats and hats on. The two mounted up behind Boone and Mason and they all raced off across the prairie, yelling and laughing.

"What the hell is that all about?" said Eden half to himself.

Minna smiled slightly. "Only time will tell."

CHAPTER FIFTEEN

The next afternoon, when Boone and Mason returned to the ranch with their brides, Eden and Minna couldn't wait to join them in celebration, and plans for the future. Two large jugs of whisky were set out in the middle of the kitchen table and everyone pulled up a chair and filled their cups.

Once the toasts were made to the happy couples, Narcissa and Leila began wondering where would be a good place to build their houses.

"Build?" said Boone.

"Houses?" said Mason.

"Well, we can't all live here on top of each other, like cats in a box," said Narcissa.

"I want a big kitchen," said Leila. "Bigger than this one."

"With lots of windows," said Minna, encouragingly.

"Absolutely," agreed Leila.

"Might have to wait till after spring round up," said Boone.

"Why wait?" Narcissa asked.

"Well, even with all the hands we hire," began Eden, "everyone of them will be needed to work the herds."

"That's right," said Mason.

"Takes a lot of men to get a big herd ready for market," said Boone.

"Just hire extra hands, and they can start on the houses," said Minna, as if solving the problem.

"That's a good idea," said Leila, all smiles.

"I agree," said Narcissa, slapping her hand on the table.

Boone and Mason looked at each other, not knowing what to say. They had assumed everything would go on as usual; they would all keep living in the main ranch house.

"There's another thing," said Eden, trying to help his brothers out of their predicament. "It's goin' to take some extra money to build two houses."

"Lots of extra money," said Boone, nodding his head for emphasis.

"Sell some horses," said Minna.

"What horses?" Eden asked.

"All those horses runnin' all over the place," replied Minna.

The three brothers stared at Minna as if she'd lost her mind.

"Minna," said Eden, softly, "it took years to raise the kind of saddle stock we got."

"How many are there?" she asked.

"A hundred of the best…" began Eden.

"Why do you need that many?" said Narcissa.

"Because…" began Boone, but Leila cut him off.

"You can't ride all of them at the same time. Right Mason?"

Looking stunned, Mason said, "Well, no, but…"

"So sell half of them," said Minna.

"Half!" said Eden, Boone, and Mason with a touch of anger.

"Can't do it," said Eden, shaking his head rapidly.

"Not my horses," said Boone, his head going as fast as Eden's.

"I raised some of them horses from the day they was foaled," said Mason to Leila, as if his heart would break.

"Oh, that's so sweet," said Leila, starting to relent.

"All right," said Minna, "then let's get some cows."

"We got cows," replied Eden.

"Thousands of 'em," added Boone.

"I meant milk cows," said Minna.

The brothers stared at Minna then glanced at each other, wondering what to do.

"With a lot of milk cows," continued Minna, "we can sell milk and butter to everybody in town, and come up with the extra money for the houses."

"Sounds good to me," said Narcissa.

"Oh, I'd love to milk some cows," said Leila. "I think it'd be fun. Huh, Mason?"

Mason simply sat there speechless.

"Milk cows wouldn't last two days out on the prairie in the winter time," said Eden.

"We'll put 'em in the barn," replied Minna.

"Not big enough," said Eden, shaking his head again.

"Yeah," added Boone. "Besides we may need to put some of the horses in there."

"Then build a bigger barn," said Minna.

"Do it the same time we build the houses," said Narcissa.

Eden sat holding his head. "You ladies don't seem to understand…"

"We'll need a bigger barn for the chickens," said Minna.

"We already got chickens," replied Eden, getting flustered.

"I mean lots of chickens," said Minna. "We can sell tons of eggs in town, along with the milk and butter."

Eden refilled his cup and took a long drink of whiskey to settle his jangled nerves. Boone and Mason did the same, their hands shaking slightly.

"We could get ourselves quite a business going," said Leila, excited. "Don't you think so, Mason?"

"I...I..." began Mason, then drained his cup and refilled it.

"And there's always pigs," said Narcissa, very business like.

The brothers looked dazed. They became even more dazed when Narcissa took a cigarette and matches out of her skirt pocket and lit up.

"I think pigs would be a good move," said Narcissa, exhaling a stream of smoke. "I don't know about anybody else here, but eating beef three times a day gets a little monotonous."

"We could have nice thick bacon for breakfast," chimed in Leila.

The brothers glanced at her and drained their cups.

"I think we're on to somethin' here," said Minna, confidently.

"Leila," said Narcissa, "you remember that group men sitting behind us on the train?"

"The drunks?"

"No, the loud mouth ones."

"Oh, yeah."

"Remember they talked about how good the wool market in Chicago is?"

"Wool?" said Eden, his eyes widening.

"What kind of wool?" asked Boone in a hostile tone.

"From sheep," said Narcissa. "What else?"

"Sheep," said Eden and Boone, springing to their feet.

"What's wrong with that?" asked Leila. "You like sheep, don't you, Mason?"

Mason could only stare down, hoping everyone would quit looking at him.

"There's plenty of room, and lots of grass, out on that old Prairie for a ton of sheep," said Minna.

"And it wouldn't be any more work than waiting for a bunch of dumb cows to grow up so you can slaughter them," said Narcissa.

"I have to agree there," added Minna.

"That's terrible, killing all those poor cows," said Leila. "Why can't you let some of them just run free, forever, like buffalo?"

Eden, Boone, and Mason sat speechless, staring at nothing in particular, trying to figure out how the three women could come up with such suggestions. Minna, Narcissa, and Leila, however, continued on about more, and better ways, to make the ranch prosper, and forgot about the three disillusioned cowboys beside them.

Late that night, with the house dark and quiet, Eden came slowly along the hallway from his and Minna's room, barefooted and wearing only his long johns. He stopped in the doorway of the kitchen, wondering if he should have a drink of coffee or whiskey. Then he noticed a glow coming from the parlor. He shuffled to the entrance and saw Boone sitting beside the fireplace. The only sound in the room came from the crackling logs. Boone didn't know anyone was there until Eden sat in the chair to his left.

"Can't sleep, huh?" said Eden, softly.

"Nope," replied Boone, just as soft.

"Me either."

"Must be the change in the weather."

"Probably."

The two remained silent, watching the flames flicker among the thick logs. Minutes later, Mason appeared and sat in the third chair near the fireplace. He was barefooted and wore only his long johns, like Eden and Boone.

"Wind's sure howlin' tonight," said Mason in a subdued voice.

"Change in the weather," said Boone.

After a moment Mason said, "That ain't all that's changin'."

The brothers looked knowingly at each other.

"Well, that's only normal, I guess," began Eden. "You get married, and, well, women being women, they got their own ideas about things."

"Sheep," said Boone, half to himself. "They want to raise sheep."

"And pigs," said Mason. "And herds of chickens."

"God help us," said Boone running his fingers through his hair.

"They're turnin' us into farmers," said Eden in a pitiful tone.

"It happened so quick," said Boone, shaking his head.

"What can we do?" Mason asked.

"Don't panic," replied Eden. "We can think our way out of this."

"They sure are full of surprises," said Mason."

Eden turned to Boone. "Did you know Narcissa smoked cigarettes?"

"Never would have dreamed it in a million years," said Boone.

"Leila smoke?" Eden asked Mason.

"Don't think so. She's just been talkin' my ear off about a big house."

"Yeah," said Boone, "Narcissa's got her whistle stuck on that, too."

"Looks like the honeymoon's comin' to an end," said Eden.

"Maybe they'll start thinkin' normal, and forget all that crazy talk," said Boone.

"They want to change things too much," said Mason. I ain't milkin' no damn cow."

"This marriage thing's all new to us," said Eden. "Could be we're over reactin'."

"Over reactin'?" said Boone. "They were talkin' about sellin' off the horses."

"I know," replied Eden. "That was pretty hard to take."

"I ain't lettin' nobody sell Rusty," said Mason with a touch of anger. "He's the best ropin' horse I ever had."

"And what about Patch?" said Boone. "He can do everything but talk."

"Settle down," said Eden. "We can't go stompin' around, and snappin' our teeth. We married good women, and they deserve to be treated with respect; no matter how crazy they think."

"I never though Leila would want to be a pig farmer," said Mason.

"I ain't gone to be able to get to sleep tonight," said Boone.

"Yes, you are," said Eden. "We all are."

"How?" asked Boone and Mason.

"We're goin' to take a step back; give the women some slack; let 'em keep talkin' and talkin', and hopefully they'll wear themselves out. Then things will return to normal."

"You might be right," said Boone. "They get to hissin' and spittin', we could be in for a rough ride."

"Sure," said Mason, enthusiastically, "let things smooth themselves out. We got to get used to this marriage stuff."

"All men do," said Eden.

"Well, I'm beginnin' to feel a lot better," said Boone.

"Me, too," said Mason, relaxing back in his chair.

"And another thing," said Eden, "we got to get ready to start bein' fathers."

"I forgot about that," said Mason, sitting forward again.

"That could be worse than raisin' sheep," said Boone, quietly.

The three brothers sat stiffly in their chairs, staring into the fire. Visions of sheep, pigs, chickens, milk cows, wives, and children danced in their throbbing heads.

Hoping to let the situation right itself, and give the women time to get their minds on other things, Eden and his brothers decided to ride south to Kilbride and look at some prize yearlings they had heard about, and maybe add them to their range stock in the spring.

Minna, Narcissa, and Leila, each with a stuffed grub bag for their man, came to the corral as Eden and his brothers finished saddling their horses.

"Got everything packed like you asked," said Minna.

"Thank you," smiled Eden, tying the bag to his saddle.

"Goin' to miss you, Mason," said Leila, handing him his grub bag.

"Won't be gone long," replied Mason, "a week, maybe."

Leila hugged him and he hugged back, giving her a gentle kiss on the lips.

"Now, don't forget," said Boone to Narcissa, "there's loaded rifles in the gun rack in the parlor, if you need 'em."

"I'll remember," said Narcissa. "Careful getting there and back," she added, kissing Boone on the cheek. He gave her a quick kiss back.

Eden mounted his horse then leaned down and kissed Minna. "I told Chunk and Billy to stop by every so often, case you need some help."

"We'll be fine," said Minna. "You come back quick."

"You can bet on it, Mrs. McKenna," said Eden, tipped his hat and rode off.

Boone and Mason followed and the three hurried galloped into the windswept prairie. The women stood watching until the three riders were barely visible then turned to each other, apprehensive at being alone in such a big, quiet stretch of country.

"Well," began Minna, a little subdued, "guess we were bound to be on our own sooner or later."

"Hope they're not going to be gone a whole week," said Leila, a bit discouraged.

"Goin' to have to keep busy till they get back." replied Minna.

"At least they didn't rear up again about our suggestions for improving things," said Narcissa.

"Oh, I figured they'd get over that," said Minna.

"So now what?" asked Narcissa.

"Let's have a cup of coffee and think on it," replied Minna.

"If we had some dogs and cats," said Leila, "I think they'd be lots of company."

"You might be right," said Minna, and the women walked towards the house discussing the idea.

CHAPTER SIXTEEN

After eight days, Eden and his brothers returned from their cattle buying trip to the south. They were happy to be getting back. They missed their wives more than they thought they would; missed the new way of life, and felt like different men now. As they rode along they could see the distant smoke plumes coming from the chimneys of the ranch house. The prairie winds were strong and biting, but the sun was bright, and long sheets of clouds drifted to the east with an urgent going. Winter was late, as if giving the land a reprieve from the harsh, unforgiving days and nights of angry blizzards, and freeze-to-death temperatures that were to come.

Getting closer to the ranch house, Eden and his brothers sensed something was different. Another change had come. Little by little they could see activity going on at the house, the bunkhouse, and the barn. Shortly, they could make out the moving shapes of the women in their bright dresses, coats and hats. And it looked as if there were lots of small, and large, shapes that had never been there before—lots and lots of shapes.

Near one of the small corrals, Leila was sitting on a low stool concentrating on the correct way to milk the large brown and white cow that was tied to a rail. Three other cows were waiting their turn, lowing in a suspicious tone, their big glassy eyes on Leila. She heard a horse neigh loudly and looked up. Through the rails of the corral she spotted the brothers approaching at a gallop.

"They're back," Leila called to Minna and Narcissa, and stood up on one of the corral rails and waved her hat excitedly.

Busy, Minna and Narcissa could only give a quick glance. Minna was carrying a large bucket of cracked corn, and walking one way then another, casting the feed left and right, followed by an endless flock of new chickens and their not so small chicks. Every direction Minna turned was a sea of feathers, along with a chorus of clucking, and a flapping of wings.

Narcissa concentrated on her own menagerie of pigs and piglets, fat and pink in the sunshine. With a long stick in one hand, and a cigarette in the other, she danced from side to side in an effort to drive the caravan of unruly pork through the open gate of a corral at the side of the barn. But the snorting, squealing brutes had other ideas.

"How come I have to do this?" shouted Narcissa to no one in particular. She stopped and took a puff on her cigarette, trying to figure out a better strategy for swine herding.

"These chickens act like they haven't eaten for a month," said Minna, flinging feed north, south, east and west.

"How long I have to keep milking?" Leila called out.

"Don't ask me," answered Narcissa, flailing away with her long stick.

"Well, my back's starting to hurt," continued Leila. "Besides, Mason's coming. I got to comb my hair."

"You can comb your hair later," ordered Minna. "Keep milkin'."

When Eden and his brothers came opposite the bunkhouse, they reined in and sat staring, not sure they were actually seeing what was in front of their eyes. The noise from the chickens, pigs, and cows were mingled chaos now. Suddenly Boone pointed to the roof of the main house. Two fat and nasty looking cats were chasing each other around one of the chimneys. A third, large and hairy lump of brown and black, lay stretched in front of the kitchen doorway, enjoying the warm rays of the noon sun.

Mason heard a squall behind him, turned and saw an even bigger cat on the roof of the bunkhouse, spinning one way then another, trying to catch its tail as if it were a matter of life and death. Then from under the front porch of the bunkhouse crawled two lanky, bony hound dogs. They squatted on their haunches and began scratching themselves violently, all the while scrutinizing the brothers and their horses with a disapproving gaze.

Finally Eden, Boone, and Mason dismounted, still trying to comprehend everything before them, and moved into the swarm and swirl of chickens, pigs, and cows. Minna hurried over to meet them.

"You got back early," she said, smiling.

"What happened?"

"Just movin' things along, like we talked about."

"But we thought you'd wait a while," replied Eden.

"We we're goin' to, then..." Minna shrugged. "How'd the cattle buyin' go?"

"Fine," said Eden, quietly, still looking around. "A herd will be brought up this spring some..."

"Well, we did some dealin' of our own, too," interrupted Minna happily.

"I can see that," said Eden.

"Where'd you get all these animals," Boone asked.

"Bought 'em from people in town."

"How?" asked Mason.

"With money, how else?"

"You had money for all this?" said Eden.

"After we sold the horses," said Minna matter-of-factly.

"What horses?" asked Eden and Mason quickly.

"The one's in the corral."

"Oh, no," said Eden, weakly.

"Say you're jokin'," pleaded Boone.

"Why?" said Minna, unconcerned.

"Rusty," said Mason, loudly, and ran towards the corral. "Rusty, boy."

"Mason," called Leila, still milking, "can you help…"

Mason paid no attention and rushed past, and through the open gate of the big corral. He stood looking one way then another. "My best horse," he shouted.

The women stared at Mason not understanding his emotional outburst.

"Mason, sweetheart," called Leila in a soothing voice, "it's only a horse for gosh sakes."

"That's right," added Narcissa, still whipping away at the milling pigs. "It's not like your right arm's been hacked off."

"Yes, it has," shouted Boone, walking towards Narcissa. "Patch is gone. He could almost spell his name in the dirt."

"Well, he should have done some spelling before we sold him," answered Narcissa, not liking Boone's tone of voice at all.

"Boone's eyes bulged. He took off his hat and flung it to the ground.

"Exactly who did you sell the horses to?" asked Eden, forcing himself to remain calm.

"Oh, some fella ridin' through," said Minna.

"When?"

"A little while after you left. Said he was vistin' all the ranches, lookin' for good cow ponies. Boone and Mason bragged on them so much we figured we could turn a profit, and then some."

Eden could only hang his head and force himself to remain quiet.

"And you spent all the money on this?" said Boone with a sweep of his arm. "Including a bunch of mangy dogs and cats?"

"That was Leila's idea," said Narcissa. "I was against it."

"I couldn't let all those poor, defenseless things end up in a stew pot, could I?" said Leila.

"What stew pot?" said Mason, testily, as he approached her.

"Well," began Leila, cheerfully, "when we were in town, I met this raggedy old man parading around with these dogs and cats, saying he was taking them home for his supper."

"Did he have real long hair and a long braided beard?" asked Mason, sternly.

"How'd you know?" said Leila, surprised.

"That was crazy Old Mose."

"Yeah," said Leila, nodding, "that's what he called himself."

"He goes around tellin' everybody he's going to eat the dogs and cats, hoping some pinhead will buy them from him."

"Wait a minute," said Leila, growing angry. "What do you mean pinhead?"

Mason turned and walked over and stood beside his brothers. Hoping to avert disaster, Minna smiled and waved her hand.

"You boys better get yourselves settled in and washed up," she said. "We'll get supper goin' soon."

Minna, Narcissa, and Leila continued with their chores, undeterred in their business ventures despite the brothers' attitude and criticism. Then, adding insult to injury, a dozen bleating sheep came stampeding out of the barn. The brothers stood open-mouthed as two scrawny dogs nipped at the heels of the panicked sheep, and drove them into the empty horse corral.

By the time supper was cooked and on the table, the women could feel a distinct chill in the air, and it wasn't from the howling wind at the windows. Eden and his brothers sat mute at their places, brooding and chewing slowly, not really tasting what they were eating. Minna, Narcissa, and Leila sneaked a glance at each other then at the brothers.

"Somethin' wrong with the food?" Minna asked softly.

"Nope," said Eden. "Fine."

"Look, Mason," Leila said sweetly. "I bought you some sweet pickles when I was in town."

Leila set the small jar beside him, smiling. Mason stared at it then spoke.

"You buy that before or after you bought the herd of dogs and cats?"

His tone was distinctly gruff, and Leila sat there in shock.

"Maybe it was after they bought the hogs and sheep," said Boone, just as gruff.

"Well," said Minna in a stern voice, "I guess some people don't welcome new ideas."

"Or appreciate what we're trying to do," added Narcissa in a sharp tone.

Eden slapped the table with both hands and sat up straight, no longer able to contain himself.

"How can we appreciate you selling our best horses, and buying sheep and hogs with the money?"

"What about some goats?" said Boone, his anger rising. "You couldn't find a couple hundred to bring back with you?"

"We were only trying to help this ranch turn a bigger profit, is all," said Minna.

"Well, don't," replied Eden.

Now it was Minna's turn to slap the table hard with both hands. She stood up and walked off down the hallway. Seconds later, the bedroom door slammed.

"Wasn't that a lovely thing to say," said Narcissa to Eden.

"Eden's right," said Boone. "You women can't go runnin' off like a brood of crazy chicken's, spendin' money left and right."

"Crazy?" said Narcissa, springing to her feet, and knocking over her chair.

"And another thing," continued Boone. "I'm not about to turn into no farmer or hog herder. So remember that."

"Don't worry, I'll remember," said Narcissa, and stormed off down the hallway.

No one said anything till after the door to her and Boone's bedroom slammed shut. Leila felt extremely uncomfortable at being left with three angry men. But she was determined to smooth things over.

"Well," said Leila, cheerfully, "guess what we're having for dessert?"

"I'm sidin' with Boone," said Mason, turning his anger on Leila. "I ain't becomin' a farmer or a milkmaid."

A hurt look came to Leila's face, she gave a muffled squeak, looking as if she were going to cry. Instead she ran to her and Mason's room and slammed the door.

The brothers remained quiet, staring down, then finally looked at each other.

"We're in for it now," said Eden.

"We had to clear the air, didn't we?" said Boone, not feeling so sure of himself anymore.

"This marriage thing is startin' to get complicated," added Mason.

"I got a feelin' this is only the beginnin'," said Eden.

Despite the heavy blankets, and heat from the wood-filled stoves, the brothers spent a chilly night in their beds, next to their equally chilly and silent spouses. And nothing had improved by sunrise the next morning.

Eden occupied his time building a fire in the cook stove. Mason went to the well to draw a bucket of water for coffee. Boone searched the shelves of the side pantry for something to eat; having the distinct feeling he wasn't going to get any breakfast unless he cooked it himself. The brothers didn't say much as they moved around the lamp-lit kitchen, grunting in answer to any questions that came up. They felt like strangers in their own house. Worse than that, they couldn't help feeling remorseful, as if they'd made a mistake somehow—but wouldn't admit it to themselves or each other.

Unconsciously, they ended up huddled at the far end of the kitchen table, discouraged and waiting for the coffee to boil. Long minutes went by then they heard a creaking of hinges, and a shuffling of slippered feet. Minna entered the kitchen, went to the crackling cook stove, checked the fire, and inserted a few more sticks of kindling.

Boone and Mason glanced at Eden, waiting for him to break the silence, but he chose to keep quiet. Boone and Mason decided that was a good idea.

Narcissa swept into the kitchen stone-faced, and wearing a long flowing robe, as if about to perform a scene from Shakespeare's McBeth. Instead she checked the coffee pot to see if it was boiling, and stood warming her backside at the stove.

Leila appeared next on swift, delicate feet, hardly making a sound. She opened the tall cupboard near the stove and began taking things down and setting them on the nearby chopping block. Without a word the three women began making breakfast.

Bacon started to sizzle; then came eggs, potatoes, slices of homemade bread, and cups of fresh milk from yesterday's milking. Then the coffee pot began to bubble and steam.

As Eden and his brothers watched they started to relax; things seemed to be returning to normal, and smelled good, too. The crisis was passing.

All they had to do was tread softly for a while; be careful of their words, and start smiling. The men winked at each other, sat up straight and cleared their throats to attract a little attention—and hopefully something to eat. But they had thought wrong.

When plates, cups and utensils were set out, it was at the opposite end of the table. Eden, Boone, and Mason waited patiently, however. When Minna, Narcissa, and Leila filled their plates and cups, and sat down, Eden's, and his brothers', hopes and expectations began to fade quickly as the women ate in silence.

Eden and Boone glanced at each other and decided to tough it out. Mason, however, began to weaken noticeably from the aroma of bacon and coffee, and Leila's angelic face, and long silky hair.

"Got anything there to share?" asked Mason, gently.

"Let me see," answered Leila, coyly; then her sparkling eyes darkened, and her expression became grim. "Oh, yes, I have those sweet pickles from town, but you don't like those, do you?" Her words were sharp and stabbing to say the least.

Mason sat stunned, as if a brick had fallen out of the sky and landed on him. His head turned slowly to Eden and Boone, but the two ignored him, worried more about their own precarious positions. Boone was about to test the cold waters surrounding Narcissa, but she beat him to it.

"I'd offer you some bacon, Boone," she said softly, then her voice became strident. "But I remember you don't like hogs or hog herding."

Boone seemed to draw into himself like a turtle in its shell.

Eden knew he was next, but was determined to take it like a man; wanting it to be over quickly, and hoping it wouldn't spoil his appetite. He watched Minna, waiting for the right time to speak, then she looked at him. Her eyes and face were empty of all life. She just stared. Eden finally broke.

"All right, all right," he yelled. "We had this comin'. You were only doin' what you thought was right. We…we acted kind of stupid."

"And hot tempered," said Boone submissively to Narcissa.

"I guess I could help milk a cow once in a while," said Mason to Leila.

The women looked at one another; their minds meeting above the kitchen table for just a split second, then the world became warm and sweet, and worth living again. Everyone moved to their usual places at the now happy table. Cups were filled and plates heaped with a breakfast that tasted especially savory, and melted in their mouths.

"You know," said Eden, cheerfully, "we shouldn't go gettin' all bent out of shape over little things like chickens and pigs, it ain't right."

Everyone agreed smilingly.

"Especially with Minna expectin' and all," added Eden proudly.

Everyone cheerfully agreed on that too. Except Minna. Her happy expression faded, and she avoided Eden's smile and set her fork down. Boone raised his cup high.

"Here's to Eden and Minna," he began, "and…"

"Wait, wait," interrupted Minna. "I…I got somethin' to say, seein' were clearin' the air about things." She pressed her lips together, trying to figure out the best way to explain. The others waited, wondering what she was up to.

"What is it, Minna?" Eden asked concerned.

"Well…the…the baby I told you about, uh…"

"Yeah?"

"I…I was wrong. I made a mistake."

"You sure?" said Eden, plainly disappointed.

"Afraid so," replied Minna, embarrassed.

There was an uncomfortable silence for a moment.

"Then why'd you hire Narcissa and Leila?" Eden asked.

Minna exchanged glances with Narcissa and Leila, giving herself time to think.

"I hired them because…well, I hired them before I found out I was mistaken about the baby."

"Lucky for us though," said Boone.

"Or we wouldn't be sittin' here with such pretty wives," added Mason.

"Yes, that's right," said Minna with relief.

"You're so sweet, Boone," said Narcissa, patting his hand.

"Nobody could ask for a smarter sister than Minna," said Leila, happily.

Every head turned to Leila, who sat there mouth open, and face pale, refusing to look at anyone.

"Sister?" said Mason, quietly.

"What do you mean, sister?" said Boone.

"You don't look like sisters," said Eden.

Boone turned to Narcissa and spoke slowly. "You mean you and…"

"Afraid so," answered Narcissa.

"You sure don't look alike," said Mason.

"Mother had quite a roving eye," said Minna. "We each had a different father."

"All of them were real nice though," Leila said with a smile.

"Mother's sort of fickeled," added Narcissa. "But lots of fun."

"Let's back up a minute," said Eden, staring hard at Minna.

Minna avoided his eyes and began eating, hoping the whole situation would disappear.

"Minna, what's goin' on?" Eden asked.

Minna looked up with a bright smile. "Oh, let's finish our wonderful breakfast and discuss all this later. It looks like it's goin' to be a nice sunny day."

"Never mind the sun," said Eden sternly. "Somethin' ain't right here."

"You know," said Boone, looking Narcissa up and down, "I'm startin' to get the same feelin'."

"What are you looking at me for?" said Narcissa. "I didn't plan any of this."

"Plan what?" asked Mason then turned to Leila. "What's she mean, plan?"

"I don't know a thing," said Leila. "You'll have to ask Minna."

"I'am," said Eden, loudly. "I'm waitin', Minna."

"All right," replied Minna, resigned to her fate. "It started off harmless enough, but I guess I got carried away."

"How?" said Eden.

"Well, I began to think about Narcissa and Leila. I hadn't seen them in such a long while, and wondered what they were up to, and thought it would be nice to get together. Then it struck me. They weren't gettin' any younger or prettier, so I…"

"What?" interrupted Leila, indignant, and looked to Mason for sympathy, but found none.

"I'm not sure I want to hear the rest of this," said Narcissa.

"Well, I do," said Eden.

"Me too," said Boone.

"And me," added Mason.

"Fine," said Minna with a shrug. "I began to think it would be nice if Narcissa and Leila could get married. Settle down before it's too late."

"You talk like we got one foot in the grave," said Narcissa.

"I'll say," said Leila.

"Now let me finish," continued Minna. "It's not as bad as you think. Once I saw Boone and Mason wanderin' around unattached, I thought what a perfect opportunity for my sisters, and my two handsome brothers-in-law. So I kept thinkin' and thinkin', and pretty soon I had a plan. If I was expectin' a baby I'd have an excuse to convince you, Eden, that hiring some help for me wouldn't be such a bad idea."

"And I fell for it," said Eden.

"Quicker than I thought. So I sent for Narcissa and Leila. In the meantime, till they got here, I pretended to go to town lookin' for help to hire. Well, they finally got here and I convinced them to keep an open mind about this marriage thing. What woman doesn't want a handsome man to marry her? Anyway, Narcissa and Leila decided to give it a go and see what developed."

"You were in on this before you even got here?" said Mason to Leila.

"I figured it wouldn't hurt to have a look around," replied Leila, sheepishly. "If you turned out to be as ugly as sin I could always get back on the train."

"That's just plain cold blooded," said Mason.

"I can hardly believe this," said Boone to Narcissa.

"Sooner or later a woman's got to start planning for her future," replied Narcissa. "Got to try for the brass ring once in a while."

"Brass ring?" said Boone. "Where, in my nose?"

"Maybe that was a bad choice of words," said Narcissa. "What I should have…"

"Don't say anymore," interrupted Boone. "This whole thing was just outright manipulation."

"Like we wasn't even human," added Mason.

"But it all turned out right in the end," said Minna. "Look at us."

"And I resent it," said Boone, getting up.

"Boone, sit down and quit acting silly," ordered Narcissa.

"Silly?" said Boone, loudly. "Now I'm silly, and got a brass ring in my nose to boot."

Forgetting his hat and coat, Boone stormed out the kitchen door slamming it behind him.

"And what about me?" Mason asked Leila. "Am I silly, too, or just a lunkhead?"

"I never said you were a lunkhead," answered Leila, defensively.

"So the silly part still sticks, does it?" said Mason, jumping up and stomping out. The bang of the kitchen door rattled the windows.

"Well," said Eden, standing up, "I guess I'm the last sheep in the pen."

"Now, Eden," said Minna, "you're lookin' at this all wrong. My intentions were…"

"You're intentions were to make me and my brothers into idiots," said Eden. "Congratulations on a job well done."

"Quit talkin' nonsense and…"

"Nonsense?" yelled Eden.

"Can't you take a joke?" Narcissa asked.

"Joke?" yelled Eden even louder.

"It does have its humorous side," said Leila.

With eyes bulging, Eden stared at Minna, waiting for her to say something contrite, but instead she burst out laughing. Then Narcissa and Leila joined in. Eden was stunned.

"Mason's right," said Eden, "this is just plan cold blooded."

Without stopping to put on his hat and coat, Eden was out the door, slamming it harder than his brothers had done. As he walked away into the chilling morning air he could still hear the women laughing. That just added to the chill.

Too mad, and too proud, to go back to the house and retrieve their hats and coats, the three brothers took shelter in the barn and paced agitatedly north, south, east and west, stopping every once in a while to kick a chicken or a wide-eyed sheep out of their way. They even yelled at a curious dog or cat that happened to saunter in. Finally Eden stopped pacing and stared grimly at his brothers.

"Did you hear that?" he asked.

"Hear what?" said Mason.

"They were laughin'."

"Laughin'?" said Boone, astounded.

"Right in my face."

"That takes a lot of gall," said Mason, shaking his head.

"They sure roped and tossed us good," said Boone, resuming his pacing.

"I never saw it comin'," said Eden, resuming his pacing. "None of it."

"What about us?" asked Mason. "Me and Boone spurred our horses all the way to town to get hitched that night."

"And practically droolin' all over ourselves," said Boone.

As Eden looked to Boone and Mason he couldn't help laughing.

"What the hell's so funny?" Boone asked.

"I can still see you and Mason ridin' out of here that night with Narcissa and Leila hangin' on behind." Eden continued laughing.

"And you think it's funny, huh?" said Mason, more upset at Eden now than at the women.

"You two really thought you'd come up with a great idea, didn't you?" Eden, laughing harder, had to lean against one of the stalls.

"What about you?" said Boone, motioning angrily at Eden. "How clever you think you are? I'll bet Minna had you jumpin' through flamin' hoops two seconds after you met her."

"Did not," said Eden, growing serious. "We hit it off nice and natural. No pretendin' at all about anything."

Mason grunted loudly. "No pretendin, huh? What about her being heavy with child?"

"You got me there," replied Eden. "She put that over good."

"Well, what are we goin' to do?" said Boone. "We can't let 'em get away with this." He put his head down and a moment later his shoulders began shaking.

"You cryin'?" asked Mason wide-eyed.

"No, you idiot," replied Boone, laughing. "I have to admit this is the best joke I ever heard pulled on anybody."

"And we were right in the middle of it," said Eden. He and Boone began laughing harder.

Mason stared at them not sure what to do, but couldn't help grinning.

"You two sound like a couple of brayin' jackasses," Mason said, his grin getting bigger and bigger, but he refused to laugh.

Eden and Boone took a minute to clam down and catch their breath.

"And they're sisters to boot," said Eden.

"Damn pretty sister," added Boone.

"Got to admire their determination," said Eden.

"Yeah, but a woman shouldn't do stuff like that," said Mason. "I'm goin' to have me a long talk with Leila, I can tell you."

"Why?" Boone asked. "She'd just look at you with those big green eyes, and wave her silky hair in your face, and you'd melt like an icicle."

Mason looked at Boone and Eden, a moment. "You're probably right."

"Come to think of it," said Eden to Boone. "We already did that with our women."

"Three weak-kneed cowboys," mumbled Boone, sadly.

"So what do we do?" Mason asked. "Slink back in the house and let 'em spur us some more? It ain't manly."

"Mason's got a point," said Boone.

Eden nodded in agreement. "But what's to be done?"

"It'll have to be good," Boone replied. "As good as what they pulled on us or it won't be worth doin'."

"Think then," said Eden.

The three brothers began their aimless pacing again; stopping once in a while to kick one of the sheep milling about them.

"I got it," said Eden. "And it'll be worth every minute, and every drop of sweat."

"What will?" asked Boone, interested.

"I'll explain on the way. Saddle up."

"Where we goin'?" Mason asked.

"See Hutch," answered Eden.

"That's a two hour ride," said Boone.

"Like I said," replied Eden, "it'll be worth every minute. And I want to pick up Chunk and Billy on the way."

"This sounds like it's goin' to be really good," said Boone, smiling.

"Better than good. Mason go get our hats, coats, and gunbelts."

"Good as done," said Mason, hurrying away.

"And don't speak to any of them women," ordered Eden.

"Don't worry," said Mason. "I wouldn't give them the satisfaction of gettin' a word out of me."

CHAPTER SEVENTEEN

It was early afternoon when Eden and his brothers, Chunk Bascom, and Billy Birdsong crossed the boundry line of Hutch Jones's huge ranch. There were horses and cattle grazing as far as you could see. Some of the herds became spooked and trotted away as Eden and the others urged their horses on towards the tight clump of buildings and corrals further out on the treeless prairie.

Twenty minutes later, the five riders reined their horses to a stop in front of the main house. The place looked deserted except for ten horses standing lazily inside a large corral, flicking their tails as they basked in the welcome warmth of the sun.

"Hello in the house," Eden called.

"Hello yourself," answered a booming voice. "Step down and come on."

"Hutch still sounds like a bull moose, don't he?" said Boone.

The others laughed, dismounted, and made their way into the big, low-ceiled log house.

Five rough looking men were seated a round a large scared table, playing cards. Suddenly they let out a wild welcome when they saw Eden and the others. After a lot of handshaking and loud back slapping, Hutch and his hired hands went on with their card game. Eden and his group pulled some extra chairs up near the table and sat down.

Hutch and his men were older than Eden and his crew, more tough and leathery looking; calloused and stiff-jointed after a lifetime of ranching, but still able to do rough cowboying when the need arose. They smoked and drank as if it were their last day on the prairies of Wyoming; and their smiles and humor were good-natured and infectious.

Hutch was king here; a stout man of medium height with muscles hard as a rock, except for his prominent potbelly produced by years of thick steaks, piles of potatoes and mountains of beans. His hair was still dark, but thin, and looked like it had never been combed, but you couldn't really tell as he always wore a big, dusty black hat which shaded his narrow gray eyes and shaggy eyebrows.

As Hutch waited for the cards to be dealt he grinned broadly at Eden, saying, "Word's goin' round you and your idiot brothers went and got married."

The rest of the card players burst out laughing.

"You heard right," said Eden.

"What'd you go and do that for?" asked one of the card players, seriously.

"Seemed like a good idea at the time," replied Boone.

"That's quite a leap of faith," said another cowhand.

"You got that right," said Mason.

"This country's hell on horses and women," said another man.

"Cattle and horses are lucky to make it through the winter, let alone a frail woman," said a third scruffy cowboy.

"The one's we got ain't exactly frail," answered Boone.

"Say," said Hutch loudly as the idea struck him, "the stove and skillets are hot from breakfast, want some grub?"

"No thanks, Hutch," replied Eden. "We came to…"

"Hang on a minute," said Hutch, "while I cheat these muskrats out of their wages, then we'll deal you fellas in."

"No offense," said Eden, "but we'll pass on that, too."

"Suit yourself," said Hutch, looking at Eden a moment, then set his cards down. "You got somethin' on your mind, don't you, cowboy?"

"A lot of somethin'," answered Eden.

"Let's have it," said Hutch.

"Well," began Eden slowly, "me, Boone, and Mason were wonderin' if you and your boys would be interested in a little shivaree?"

The rest of the card players quickly became interested and waited for Eden to continue.

"Chunk and Billy, here, are all for it," continued Eden. "I thought maybe you boys would be, too."

"What kind of a shivaree?" Hutch asked.

"And who's it for?" added one of the cowboys.

"Our women folk," answered Eden. "You see they're from back east, and…"

"At least we think they are," interrupted Boone.

"Right now we're not too sure where they came from," said Mason.

Hutch and his men glanced at each other, puzzled.

"Anyway," Eden went on, "being city girls, we kind of wanted to get them used to livin' in the wild and woolly west. Initiate them, so to speak."

"Yeah," said Boone, "somethin' they'll never forget."

"For as long as they live," said Mason.

A smile came to Hutch's leathery face and he nodded. "That could be real interestin'."

It'd sure relieve the monotony of sitting around here day after day," added one of the men.

"And give us something to laugh about when we're snowed in later," said another cowboy.

"But we need to do it quick," said Eden. "And do it right."

"We're the men for the job," said Hutch, banging his gnarly fist on the table.

"These all the hands you got?" asked Eden, motioning to the card players.

"Another bunch is in town," replied Hutch. "Be back in the mornin'."

"That's when I want to do this," said Eden.

"I like it already," said Hutch, pounding on the table again. "Jubal, open up a fresh bottle of rat poison, so we can think better; oil our minds up."

The scruffy looking cowboy to Hutch's right reached down and brought up a quart bottle of whiskey and proceeded to fill all available cups and glasses, while Eden laid out his plan for the shivaree.

Eden and his brothers returned to the ranch later than anticipated. The moon was just rising, and the wolves, hunting on the prairie, were calling one another. The brothers unsaddled inside the barn, gave their horses a rubdown, and a good feed then turned in.

The ranch house was dark, but the men welcomed the soothing warmth after their long, cold ride, and raucous meeting with Hutch. They had worked out every last detail for what was to take place tomorrow morning.

Quietly, the brothers slipped under the bed covers beside their wives, closed their eyes in contentment, and a smile on their faces.

CHAPTER EIGHTEEN

The sun was just cracking the horizon when Mason came stomping out of the brightly lighted kitchen and down the long hallway to the bedrooms. He began hammering his fist on the each of the bedroom doors, then turned and stomped back towards the kitchen, his spurs ringing loudly.

"Come and get it," he shouted. "Or I'm throwin' it out!"

Minna, Narcissa, and Leila finally emerged from their rooms still half asleep, hair all frizzled, and their flannel robes draped over their heavy nightgowns. All three were puzzled as to what was going on. When they reached the kitchen they found Eden and Boone fixing breakfast, and arguing how to cook everything. Mason was whistling merrily as he neatly set the table.

"There's them frisky little fillies now," said Boone, happy and smiling.

"Set right down," said Mason, "and make yourselves comfortable."

The women glanced at each other, wondering if they were in the right house, but sat down anyway.

"You're not the only one's know how to cook," said Eden with a broad smile. "I'm fixin' plenty for everybody."

"Coffee be ready in a second," added Boone.

"What happened to you boys last night?" Minna asked. "We got worried."

"Oh, just got caught out there late, countin' steers," answered Boone. "Nothin' serious."

Mason hurried over to the table with the steaming coffee pot, and began filling Leila's cup.

"Here go, sweetheart," he said. "Don't burn them pretty lips now."

Leila beamed and ran her fingers through Mason's hair. "You're so sweet to me."

"And you deserve it," said Mason, starting to fill Minna's and Narcissa's cups.

"Isn't he sweet?" Leila said to her sisters.

Minna and Narcissa eyed Mason a moment then looked to Eden and Boone still fussing around the cook stove.

"You all were awful mad when you left here yesterday," said Minna, suspiciously.

The brothers laughed loudly.

"That was yesterday," said Eden. "Today's today." He tossed a flapjack into the air and caught it in the skillet.

"So we don't have to hide our heads in shame anymore?" Narcissa asked.

"You just keep that pretty head where I can see it," said Boone, setting a plate of flapjacks in front of her. "I'm warmin' up some syrup, darlin', won't be long."

A big smile came to Narcissa's face. "I could enjoy eating breakfast like this every morning."

The breakfast turned into a major success. The brothers waited on the sisters hand and foot, and then some. Minna and her sisters began to feel like queens, and all the past lies and dirty tricks were forgotten—at least by them. A new chapter was begun in the book of matrimonial happiness.

The praise and caring attitudes of the brothers didn't stop after breakfast, it went right on into the bright, sunny outdoors. But not without a gritting of teeth, and swallowing of pride. Cowboy work was put aside and other chores given first place.

Eden found himself sweating, sawing and hammering, as he helped Minna at the rear of the barn. The two began constructing a large pen for the rooting, snorting pigs and piglets surrounding them. Eden even managed to smile when Minna decided the pan needed and extra rail along the bottom. More measuring, sawing, hammering and sweating caused him to remove his hat and coat. However, he refused to hang up his gunbelt, or set aside the extra revolver that was tucked securely in the front of the belt.

Inside the barn, their hats and coats off, but gunbelts and extra revolvers at their waists, Boone and Mason sweated under female orders. Boone was wielding a heavy sledge hammer; knocking down the walls of one of the horse stalls to make more room for the mob of milling, bleating sheep that seemed to be worshipping Narcissa as she talked and petted them. Boone paused and mopped his face with his big red bandana.

"You sure these woollies need this much space?" he asked.

"You can't expect them to lay on top each other like sardines in a can," replied Narcissa.

"I don't care how they sleep," mumbled Boone, pounding away again with this sledge hammer.

"What?" said Narcissa, looking up from the sheep.

"I said, why can't they sleep outside, dear?"

"What if a blizzard comes, silly?"

"That's why they're covered with wool, ain't it?"

"And knock down that post behind you," ordered Narcissa.

"You want the barn to collapse?"

"It won't fall down," replied Narcissa, and turned her loving attention to the sheep.

Boone started to say something then thought better of it. He made sure Narcissa wasn't looking, and kicked the nearest sheep, sending it bawling towards the far end of the barn, where Mason labored under the affectionate gaze of Leila.

He chewed his lower lip hard to keep from saying anything off-color as he bent low on a stool, milking the largest and most contentious of the three milk cows. Suddenly he sat up straight, his face shiny with sweat, and his back aching.

"Isn't that enough?" he asked, making it sound more like and order than a question.

Leila looked into the bucket and shook her head. "I get way more than that. Keep milking."

Mason's eyes glared with frustration and anger. He could no longer control himself, was about to saying something, when the large, hairy tip of the cow's tail swatted him hard in the face. He sat back quickly, his hand grabbing his revolver, but Leila didn't notice that; she was too busy laughing.

Though the pig pen still needed more work, Minna was herding the troop of swine inside it to make sure the future moneymakers would have plenty of room to spread out and prosper. Unable to stand much more, Eden excused himself, saying he needed a drink of water. At a brisk walk, he headed for the well, near the house.

As he reeled the bucket up on its rope, he mumbled many unkind words about pigs in general. Calming himself, somewhat, he noticed Chunk Bascom and Billy Birdsong galloping in. He set the water bucket down and hurried to meet them. Chunk and Billy reined their horses to a stop, looking eagerly around the ranch.

"Nobody here yet, huh?" said Chunk, quietly.

"Won't be long," answered Eden. "You boys ready?"

The two reached into the pockets of their long coats and brought out a heaping handful of blank revolver cartridges.

"Ready for the warpath," said Billy, grinning.

"Go on in the house," said Eden. "Coffee's on the stove. But keep your eyes and ears open."

"Don't worry," said Chunk, bright eyed, "I wouldn't miss this for a barrel of whiskey."

Having had their fill of pigs, sheep, and milk cows, Eden and Boone talked the sisters into working on the winter wood supply. More still needed to be split and stacked along the entire rear of the main house. Mason, however, took a long ladder and climbed up on the house roof, to inspect for loose shingles, he told Leila. But his real intention was to watch the horizon to the south.

"I thought I saw Chunk and Billy ride in," said Minna, colleting some kindling.

"Guess they're still in the house swilling coffee," replied Eden, swinging his heavy axe.

"Company comin'," Mason called out.

Everyone looked to Mason who stood at the peak of the house roof, pointing south. A few seconds passed then a group of horsemen began to take shape far out on the dark grass of the prairie. Minna and her sisters stood watching, wondering who it could be. Eden and Boone began walking casually away. Mason climbed down from the roof and joined his brothers, now moving towards the large corral beside the barn. At the same time, Chunk and Billy came to a rear corner of the main house and stood quietly.

When the riders drew closer, they reined their horses to a walk and spread out in a long line abreast. Minna and her sisters could count ten men; each with a rifle or shotgun held in their right hand. Minna turned to say something to Eden and saw he was gone. She turned around further and saw him, Boone, and Mason standing by the big corral, their hands on their revolvers.

"Who are they, Eden?" Minna called, starting to feel uncomfortable.

"Too soon to tell," answered Eden.

"Don't look very friendly," said Narcissa to herself.

"Sure have a lot of guns," said Leila. "Must be out hunting."

With their horses still moving at a walk, Hutch Jones and his rough looking cowboys had an aura of doom about them; their faces blank as stone, eyes cold and unblinking. Hutch held up a hand and the riders stopped not far from the women. Minna and her sisters started to smile then changed their minds as the unshaven, scruffy men eyed them grimly, then looked to Eden and his brothers.

"Mornin', McKenna," said Hutch in a somber tone.

Eden just nodded. Boone and Mason gripped their revolvers tighter.

"We had a long, cold ride from town," continued Hutch, his jaw barely moving, "so I ain't goin' to waste no words. The sheriff deputized me, and these men, and ordered us to bring you in."

Minna, Narcissa, and Leila turned their attention to their husbands, waiting for an explanation.

"Now that don't sound very friendly," said Boone.

"You sure you got the right fellas?" added Mason, sarcastically.

"Every rancher around here is tired of you boys stealin' their stock," answered Hutch.

Shocked, Minna and her sisters stood there with mouths open. Minna finally swallowed and said: "What's he talkin' about, Eden?"

"What'd you get us into?" Narcissa whispered to Minna.

"You telling me I married a cow thief?" said Leila.

"Like you three didn't know," said Hutch, loudly.

"No, we didn't," answered Minna.

"You three look onery enough to be cattle thieves yourselves," replied Hutch.

The sisters glanced at each other, not knowing what to say.

"And you're comin' along, too," said Hutch, pointing at Chunk and Billy, still leaning against the corner of the house.

"I don't think so," said Chunk, and he and Billy stood up straight, putting hands on their revolvers.

Hutch motioned to the women, saying, "You riffraff better step aside."

"Riffraff?" said Minna, insulted and angry.

Narcissa turned to Boone. "You going to let him talk to me like that?"

"Don't pay no attention to the dirty dog," replied Boone.

"Mason," said Leila, her temper rising, "why don't you say something?"

"Not right now, sweetheart."

"Well," said Hutch, rising tall in his saddle, "I guess things area about to turn ugly."

"Your call, lawman," said Eden, calmly.

"Wait a minute," said Minna. "Can't we talk this out? No sense gettin'..."

That was as far as Minna got in her plea. Eden, Boone, and Mason drew their revolvers and began shooting. Hutch and his men returned fire, their rifles and shotguns blasting dense clouds of gun smoke over the heads of the women.

"You women get in the barn," yelled Eden, backing away, shooting.

Minna and her sisters started for the barn as fast as they could go, then Boone yelled for them to get in the house. They turned and ran in that direction. Eden yelled again for them to get in the barn. Minna and Narcissa paid no attention; the roar of the gunfire and the plunging, bucking horses were all they were conscious of. However, Leila did a quick turnaround and raced into the barn and leaped behind a pile of stuffed feed sacks. Her head bobbed back up, and her bugged-out eyes stared towards the open front doors. The sound of gunfire and yelling had increased.

"Jesus, Mary, Joseph," gasped Leila. "What'd I marry into?"

Seconds later, she heard loud voices and the jingling of spurs. Two armed men came through the open rear doors of the barn. All the sheep, and the three milk cows, ran ahead of the men and out the front doors, bleating, bawling, and leaping.

"Where the hell all them sheep come from?" said one of the scruffy looking cowboys.

"Damned if I know," replied the other. "Sure stink, don't they?"

Leila sprang up from behind the feed sacks, her hands raised high. "Don't shoot, I give up," she shouted.

The two cowboys jumped to one side, scared by her shout.

"What are you tryin' to do," yelled the oldest man, "turn my hair white?"

"Sorry," said Leila, her hands still raised. "I didn't mean..."

"Just stay like you are," ordered the oldest man.

"Or we'll hang you right now," added the younger cowboy.

"Oh, God," said Leila in a faint, squeaky voice.

The younger cowboy then smiled and tipped his hat, saying, "You sure are a pretty heifer."

"Never mind that," said the older cowboy. "We got to go kill somethin'."

"Right."

The two men hurried towards the front of the barn when two cowboys, on horseback, rode into view, stopped, and began shooting in the direction of the ranch house. Suddenly they fell from their horses. Their loud cries were drowned out by the increasing gunfire.

"They got Curley and Baldy," shouted the older cowboy.

"The dirty bushwhackers," yelled the younger cowboy. "Let's get 'em."

The two ran out of the barn firing their revolvers wildly, then fell to the ground.

"Oh, my God," whimpered Leila, seeing what had happened. She slowly sank behind the pile of feed sacks, her hands still raised.

Eden, Boone, and Mason were now crouched behind the rails of the big corral, shooting and yelling at Hutch and his men as they rode by, shooting back. Eden turned to Boone and Mason, saying, "Why don't one of you fall down?"

"Why don't you?" said Boone, still shooting.

"I'm having too much fun," replied Eden.

"Well, so are we," said Mason, starting to reload his revolver.

"Where'd Chunk and Billy get to?" asked Eden.

"There they are," answered Mason, motioning to the bunkhouse.

Chunk and Billy stood on the roof of the bunkhouse, firing their revolvers, and cursing four riders, who raced by below them. The four returned fire with their shotguns.

"Guess it's time to go to the happy huntin' ground," said Chunk.

"Right behind you," said Billy.

Both men emptied their revolvers as more riders passed by, yelling and firing their rifles. Chunk staggered backwards, made sure he wasn't too close to the edge of the roof, and fell down. Billy gave an Indian war cry and fell beside him.

Inside the kitchen of the ranch house, Minna and Narcissa were crouched low in a corner of the thick protective log walls. They hugged each other as the yelling and shooting continued nearby.

"Sounds like the Battle of Gettysburg," said Narcissa.

Minna raised up cautiously, and peeked out a window. In the swirl of gun smoke and dust, she could just make out men on foot, and horseback, moving in every direction.

"I see Eden and Boone," Minna said excitedly

Narcisssa jumped up and looked out the window. "Where?"

"Over there."

Narcissa squinted, trying to see through the drifting wall of dust. Three cowboys ran past the window, shooting towards the big corral.

"None of them can shoot very good," said Narcissa.

"Don't be so sure?" replied Minna. "Look on the bunkhouse roof."

"Oh, my God," said Narcissa, when she saw Chunk and Billy lying there.

"Satisfied now?" Minna asked.

"Me?" replied Narcissa, her anger rising. "If you hadn't talked me and Leila into marrying into a bunch of cattle thieves, I wouldn't be getting shot at."

"Well, they're still our husbands," said Minna. "For better or for worse."

"I didn't expect the worse this soon," replied Narcissa.

Three cowboys, on horseback, milled around close to the window, firing their revolvers. Minna and Narcissa ducked down, covering their heads with their hands.

Narcissa looked up suddenly, saying, "Do you know if they had their wills made out?"

"What the hell's wrong with you?" Minna yelled.

"I'm just thinking ahead, is all," answered Narcissa.

At the outside of the kitchen door stood two cowboys, laughing softly. One poured dark, sticky molasses out of a bottle into the cupped hand of the other, who said, "Can't wait to see their faces."

"I peeked in, and they're hiding in the far corner," said the other cowboy, and poured the rest of the molasses into his free hand, and tossed the bottle away. "Ready?"

"Let 'ere rip."

The two rubbed the molasses on their faces and shirt fronts, then kicked open the kitchen door.

Minna and Narcissa rose slowly, mouths gapping, as the two men staggered in. The men stared at Minna and Narcissa with crazy eyes, molasses dripping from their faces and hands like blood; their shirt fronts dark with it.

"I'm too young to die," whined the first cowboy, and dropped to the floor.

"And I'm younger than he is," whined the second, and raised a cloud of dust when he hit the floor.

Narcissa looked at Minna, saying, "You still going to tell me what wonderful husbands we have?"

"I guess not," said Minna, staring at the two bloody bodies.

Hutch and another cowboy appeared at the open kitchen door, guns pointed. They glanced at the two molasses soaked men, then to Minna and Narcissa.

"You do that?" Hutch asked angrily.

"No," said Minna loudly.

"They were dead when we got here," added Narcissa.

"Don't try nothin' or I'll drill both of you," snarled Hutch, waving his revolver.

The other cowboy, however, smiled and nodded as he looked the two women up and down. "Nice to meet you," he said politely. "You ladies ain't busy later, maybe…"

"Hey, hey," interrupted Hutch, "stick to business. Get out there and shoot somebody."

The cowboy tipped his hat to Minna and Narcissa, and went out the door, shooting right and left at nothing in particular.

"I feel sorry for you women when this is over," said Hutch. "The law hangs cattle thieves; male or female."

"We're entitled to a lawyer," said Narcissa.

"The only lawyer in town got killed in a bar fight," replied Hutch.

"We're entitled to a fair trial," said Minna angrily.

"Don't hold your breath on that one," replied Hutch.

Then, the cowboy Hutch had sent outside staggered back in. He was holding his stomach and his face was contorted in pain. "They got me," he gasped. "They got me bad."

"Well, don't whine about it," said Hutch. "Be a man."

"You're right," replied the cowboy. "I'm goin' out fightin'."

He staggered out, and past the kitchen window, firing his revolver, then staggered backwards. Hutch, Minna, and Narcissa watched in amazement as the cowboy kept staggering and shooting, and crying out, pretending he was getting hit by one bullet after another. Finally he fell by the kitchen door, flinched a few times and lay still.

Hutch turned to the women. "Old Jeb, there, was sure a tough one," said Hutch proudly.

"Wasn't very smart," replied Narcissa.

"What?" yelled Hutch.

"What's wrong with you people," said Minna. "Why don't you act like real men and…"

"Real men?" shouted Hutch, taking a step towards Minna. "I'll show you real men, missy."

Hutch went to the kitchen door and stuck his head out. "Hold your fire," he shouted. "Hold your fire, damn it!"

Gradually the shooting ceased.

"McKenna," called Hutch. "Eden McKennan!"

"I hear you," replied Eden from the far corner of the bunkhouse.

"Let's quit playin' run-around," said Hutch. "Let's settle this like real men."

"Sounds fine to me," Eden yelled back. "Come on out!"

"I'm comin'!"

Minna and Narcissa looked out one of the kitchen windows as Hutch moved across the porch and into the dusty, body-littered yard. Leila came running in the rear door of the house, and down the long hallway past the bedrooms to the kitchen. Her face and dress were covered with dirt and dust, and her hair all tangled with straw.

"Thank God you're alive," said Leila when she saw her sisters.

"What in hell happened to you?" Minna asked.

"I crawled all the way from the barn, There's bodies all over hell out there."

"They aren't all out there," replied Narcissa, motioning to the two cowboys sprawled on the kitchen floor.

"Oh, my God," said Leila, then hurried to one of the kitchen windows. "What they doing now?"

"Being real men," answered Narcissa in a sarcastic tone.

"There's my poor Mason," said Leila. "What can we do?"

"Get a divorce," said Narcissa.

"But isn't the widow entitled to some property or something?" Leila asked.

"I swear," said Minna, loudly, "you two are the most mercenary females I ever met."

"Well, you got us into this," said Leila.

"I already told her that," said Narcissa, lighting a cigarette.

Minna turned back to the window. "There comes the rest of them," she said.

Narcissa and Leila looked out and saw Hutch, and his two remaining cowboys, walking slowly towards the bunkhouse. Eden, Boone, and Mason stood waiting, their guns holstered.

The two groups watched each other closely. When they were only ten yards apart, Hutch and his men stopped, hands on their revolvers.

"You got one more chance to give up," said Hutch.

"Can't hear you," replied Eden.

"Me either," said Boone.

"Hold on," said Mason with a look of concern. "I need some bullets."

"Well, get some," yelled Hutch.

"You got any more?" Mason asked his brothers, and they began searching their pockets.

Hutch impatiently tapped his dusty boot against the ground. The cowboy on Hutch's right started rolling a cigarette, while the cowboy on Hutch's left took a pint bottle of whiskey from his coat pocket, and took a quick swig.

"Put that away," ordered Hutch. "You're an officer of the law for Pete's sake."

"My throat's dry," replied the cowboy.

"It's always dry," grumbled Hutch then turned his attention to Eden and his brothers. "You three are the sorriest bunch of cattle thieves I ever did see."

"Hang on a minute," said Eden as he and Boone continued searching their pockets.

"You have any extra bullets?" Mason asked Hutch.

"We ain't givin' you any damn bullets, lame brain," shouted Hutch.

"Don't have to get insultin'," replied Mason.

"Here's three," said Eden, handing Mason some blank cartridges.

"I got two," said Boone, tossing them to Mason.

As Mason loaded his revolver, Eden and Boone noticed Minna and her sisters looking out the kitchen window, and waved to them. The women could only stare back dumbfounded.

"You ready?" Hutch asked irritated.

"Ready you old gopher," answered Mason, shoving his revolver into his holster.

"Make your play," said Eden, staring hard at Hutch.

All six men tensed, hands touching their guns. They waited for someone to make the first move. Minna, Narcissa, and Leila were still watching, their hands pressed to their faces.

A split second later, the men drew their revolvers. The firing was loud and quick. The two cowboys with Hutch were the first to fall, then came

Mason and Boone, then Hutch and Eden. The last of the revolver shots echoed across the prairie, and disappeared in the whisper of the wind.

With all the courage that was in them, Minna, Narcissa, and Leila left the safety of the ranch house and walked slowly out onto the silent battlefield. Bodies were lying in every direction; riderless horses milled here and there; sheep huddled nervously in the big corral, bleating, and the milk cows wandered aimlessly, bawling loudly. A few dogs and cats made a cautious appearance, sniffing and looking, trying to figure out what all the yelling and noise had been about.

The sisters came to within a few feet of Eden, Boone, and Mason, and stared down at their lifeless bodies.

"I can't believe this," said Minna, softly. "Eden had his good points, even for a two-bit cow thief."

Narcissa wiped a tear from her eye before she spoke. "Boone never said an unkind word to me. At least not any I didn't deserve."

"My Mason," said Leila, a hand to her mouth. "So young to die this way. But I guess it's better than having your neck stretched."

"I wonder who gets the ranch?" Narcissa said half to herself.

"Narcissa, you quit that," yelled Minna.

"I was wondering that, too," said Leila.

It was right then they heard laughing. The women turned quickly and saw Chunk and Billy sitting on the edge of the bunkhouse roof, looking down and laughing. Then there was more laughter. The women kept turning one way then another as Hutch and all his cowboys began sitting up. Finally Eden, Boone, and Mason did the same. Some of the nearby horses were shaking their heads and seemed to be laughing too.

As the shock and confusion wore off, Minna and her sisters realized they had been the butt of a little cowboy humor. But it didn't set too well just then. They began heaping unkind words on their husbands, who could only laugh harder, until the women came at them with a vengeance. Eden and his brothers jumped up and ran, and squirmed their way through the rails of the big corral. The women started to climb over after them.

"Now hold on, Minna," said Eden. "You got to admit you three deserved every minute of this."

"That was the worst thing a human being ever did to another human being," shouted Minna.

"You mean it's worse than the trick you and your sisters pulled on us?" Boone asked.

"Well, I...I..." Minna could think of nothing to say, and looked at Narcissa.

"He's right," said Narcissa. "We asked for this."

"They made me go along with all their crazy ideas," Leila said to Mason.

"I believe you, sweetheart," replied Mason, smiling.

"I'm glad you aren't dead," said Leila. "I don't look very good in black."

"Neither do I," answered Mason, and climbed up onto the corral and gave her a kiss.

Minna and Narcissa sat on the top rail looking down at Eden and Boone.

"Well?" said the two sisters.

Eden and Boone smiled and held out their arms. The two women jumped from the corral into their arms.

It didn't take long for some dancing and drinking to be organized—sort of a belated wedding reception, western style. The big kitchen of the ranch house was cleared of all tables and chairs. Hutch and his cowboys, Chunk and Billy, along with Eden and his brothers, Minna and her sisters, formed a circle around the room. A loud harmonica and a twangy Jew's harp opened the ball.

Stomping boots, jingling spurs, and clapping hands accompanied Leila as she proceeded to dance with each eagerly awaiting cowboy. Jugs of whiskey were passed around to keep things festive. Leila was nearly out of breath, and weak in the knees, when she completed her dance-around. She called for Narcissa to relieve her. With a cheerful shout Narcissa did a graceful spin into the center of the floor to where Hutch waited, grinning and stamping both feet; like we was ready to run a race.

Leila hung onto Mason with both arms, gave a deep sigh and looked up at him.

"You still in love, cowboy?" she asked.

"I sure am," said Mason.

"So am I. And I haven't forgotten about that house you promised me."

"You'll have it. And in the parlor there should be a big window. Real big. So we can look out and see all those thousands of fat, sassy steers, and hundreds of shiny horses with their tail streamin' in the wind."

"Don't forget the milkers," added Leila.

"The what?"

"Milk cows. I'm starting to get the hang of it, and figure we can use some more."

"Then milk cows you'll have."

"And a really big garden."

"You're bound and determined to turn me into a farmer, ain't you?"

"No. Just the best husband a woman ever had."

"That could take a lifetime."

"I sure hope so," said Leila with a big, bright smile.

Mason took her in his arms and held her tight.

As Narcissa came spinning her way around the room, in the arms of a new partner, she called to Minna to rescue her. Minna took her place and danced away. Narcissa wrapped her arms around Boone and rested her head on his shoulder.

"I'm awful fond of you, pretty lady," Boone whispered.

Narcissa ran her fingers through his hair, saying, "And I'm getting quite fond of you, Mr. McKenna."

"Course I'm still not to fond of them sheep," said Boone.

"They are starting to become a bit of a nuisance."

"Maybe we should sell 'em to a sheepherder."

"The quicker the better."

"Besides," said Boone, holding her tight, "in a few years you won't have time for sheep. This ranch will be so big you'll be busy figurin' out how to spend all the money floodin' in."

"I could get used to that. And don't forget a really big house. And a cook too, I think."

"Whatever you heart desires, Mrs. McKenna. Just tell me."

"I will."

Hutch and the other cowboys let out a wild war cry when they spotted Boone and Narcissa in a long, passionate kiss.

"Leila," called Minna with a wave of her arm.

"Leila plunged back onto the dance floor, and whirled away with a high-stepping Billy Birdsong.

Minna leaned heavily on Eden and he gave her a long, warm kiss.

"Well, Minna, my love, here we are. Seems like a new start; like the first time we met."

"Feels good, don't it?" said Minna.

"We're goin' to have a great life."

"I'm plannin' on it."

"Then plan ahead and don't look back."

"And let's not forget the baby."

"You ain't startin' that again, are you?"

"Yes. But this time it's the truth."

Eden's eyes widened as Minna nodded her confirmation. He let out a yell, took Minna in his arms and danced into the circle of cowboys. Boone and Narcissa joined them. Mason ran to Leila, stealing her away from Billy. As the three couples sashayed around and around the room, Hutch and the others hollered and clapped, in time to the music, and their heavy boots created a thunder against the plank flooring.